# Anywhere
# But Here

# Anywhere But Here

## Adele Dueck

NORTHERN
LIGHTS YOUNG NOVELS

Red Deer College Press

*The Publishers*
Red Deer College Press
56 Avenue & 32 Street Box 5005
Red Deer Alberta Canada T4N 5H5

*Acknowledgments*
Edited for the Press by Tim Wynne-Jones.
Cover Art and Design by Jeff Hitch.
Text design by Dennis Johnson.
Printed and bound in Canada by WebCom Limited for Red Deer College Press.
The author acknowledges the support of the Saskatchewan Arts Board during the writing of this book.

5 4 3 2 1

Financial support provided by the Alberta Foundation for the Arts, a beneficiary of the Lottery Fund of the Government of Alberta, and by the Canada Council, the Department of Canadian Heritage and Red Deer College.

COMMITTED TO THE DEVELOPMENT OF CULTURE AND THE ARTS

*Canadian Cataloguing in Publication Data*
Dueck, Adele, 1955–
Anywhere but here
(Northern lights young novels)
ISBN 0-88995-147-0
I. Title. II. Series.
PS8557.U28A75 1996   jC813'.54   C95-911206-5
PZ7.D83An 1996

*For my parents, Frank and Lona Loken*

# Anywhere But Here

# PROLOGUE

*T*HE STILLNESS OF THE PRAIRIE NIGHT WAS BROKEN BY AN EERIE, GRATING *sound that made my scalp tingle and goose bumps rise on my arms. Rodos growled deep in his throat, and I put my hand on his head so he'd know I was there and not be frightened.*

*The sound lasted only seconds. It had barely died away when I heard a vehicle start up. It seemed to come closer. There was a noise like a car door slamming, and then the motor faded away.*

*The night was silent again, except for the croaking of the frogs from the dugout and another low growl from Rodos.*

*Pulling him with me, I edged backward till I was pressing against the handle of the porch door. I hadn't turned on any lights when I'd crept downstairs to see why the dog was barking, and the sliver of a moon was no help at all. I peered in the direction of the noise, past the darkness that was Dad's shop and the smaller shadow of the bunkhouse, out of the yard, into the blackness beyond.*

*"Must be someone down on the highway," I whispered. My arm slipped around Rodos' shoulder, and I knelt beside him on the step. After all, where else could the sound have come from? The nearest farm was a mile away, and no one lived there. It had to have come from the highway. Maybe someone had a flat tire, and the noise was the jack scraping across the pavement.*

*Rodos didn't seem to believe that any more than I did. Instead of relaxing, he stiffened and growled again.*

*I shivered, feeling suddenly cold, though the June night was warm. It was time to go back to bed anyway, if I wanted to be awake for my last day in grade five. I gave Rodos another hug, and his ears pricked up as if he had something to say. Then he took off across the yard, barking as loudly as when he woke me a short while before.*

*Though I had no idea what he was barking at, it was comforting to know he was there, guarding the farm, keeping us safe.*

# CHAPTER 1

"**M**ARJORIE!"

It was Mum calling in the voice that said she'd already called three times.

"Come help with supper."

I groaned and stretched and turned the page in my book. Why me? Trevor and Nick could help just as well as I could. Better. There were two of them.

"Marjorie, do you want me to come and get you?"

Not exactly.

I left *Mystery Lights at Blue Harbour* unsolved on my bed, right beside the letter I'd tried to write to Pam. A boring letter, which was why I'd stopped writing and read my book instead. So far all it said was, "Dear Pam, I don't know how I'll get through a whole summer without you."

I lifted the door as I closed it so the latch would catch, then, to be sure Mum knew I'd hurried, flew down the stairs two at a time.

"What took you so long?" she demanded as I rushed into the kitchen. "Just because school's out doesn't mean you get to read all day. You know I'm trying to finish that dress for Mrs. Geller, and now I have one to make for Lois Cranston as well." She held out a head of cabbage, but I ignored it and threw my arms around her.

"That's terrific! At this rate, you'll make tons of money."

"Don't I wish," she said. She continued turning sausages with one hand while holding the cabbage in the other.

I started to take the cabbage, but Mum pulled it back. "Did you wash your hands?"

I ran water over them in the kitchen sink and watched a fly swirl down the drain with the water.

"Next time try soap and a basin," suggested Mum. I was glad she didn't notice me dry my hands on the seat of my shorts.

Though I chopped the cabbage as carefully as I could, I still seemed to get more on the floor than in the bowl. "You should see the food processor Lisa's mum has," I said, kicking a chunk away from my feet. "We did a whole cabbage in about one minute, and there was no mess."

"Great idea," said Mum. "Next time you need shoes or underwear, I'll put the money toward a food processor instead."

"On the other hand," I went on, ignoring her, "Lisa did say it was a pain to clean the machine afterward."

"Good, then we won't get one." Mum stepped outside to call the twins to set the table. "It wouldn't have been a good idea, anyway," she added as she brought over carrots for the salad. "I would have felt really guilty sending you to school with your toes sticking through the holes in your shoes."

She took over making the salad, so I went to put on water for tea. My reflection in the shiny curve of the kettle looked even worse than usual. I pulled a face, but the kettle made an uglier one back at me.

"If it looks that bad," said Mum, "you can always polish it."

"My face?" I said, surprised, but then realized she meant the kettle. It did have a few fingerprints and was splattered with something that may or may not have been tomato soup. I didn't think it would keep the water from boiling, though, so I set it on the stove the way it was.

"How come Angie has beautiful blonde curls and I'm stuck

with this?" I grabbed a handful of my plain brown hair and gave it a painful tug.

"Never mind," said Mum. "By the time she's eleven, she'll probably have straight brown hair, too."

"The poor kid. Her future's ruined and she's only three."

"Brown hair isn't so bad," said Mum, probably thinking of her own brown waves. "The boys don't seem to mind."

I glanced over to where Trevor and Nick were practically throwing dishes on the table in their hurry to be done. Nick was coated in a layer of grease he'd collected while helping Dad in the shop.

Of course they didn't care. They were boys . . . and seven years old. They'd probably be happiest with their heads shaved. Then they wouldn't have to waste time brushing.

"If I dyed my hair and got a perm—" I began but didn't get any further. Mum made a short sound that might have been a laugh, Nick hooted and Trevor asked very sensibly, "Where are you going to get the money?"

That was the problem, of course, and I looked at Mum. Her expression wasn't promising.

"Get the milk out of the fridge, Nick, and stop making that ridiculous noise." She poured boiling water into the teapot and set it on the table. I watched.

"Goodness, Marjorie, would you please help get supper on the table and stop standing there like a bump. It's ten past six already, and you know your father likes his meals on time."

"But what about my hair?"

"Your hair looks fine just as it is. Besides, if you got a perm, it would be gone in no time. You know how quickly your hair grows. And don't start bothering your father about this. He's got enough to worry about."

She didn't say anything about dyeing my hair, and I didn't mention it again. It wasn't hard to guess what her answer would be. But when I get a job and make my own money . . .

Our hired man came in for supper just as Dad finished saying grace. Larry had only been working for us a couple of months. He didn't talk a lot or spend much time with us, except at meals, so I didn't know him very well—not like our last hired man, who'd been with us for years and seemed like an uncle. Larry dropped his dirty blue cap on Angie's head as he pulled out the chair beside her, then ran his hand through his reddish blond hair, making it stand up on end. If I had hair that color, I'd never be jealous of Angie.

"Finish that field?" asked Dad.

"Not quite," said Larry. "Had some troubles, but I should get done in the morning."

"How about this evening?" suggested Dad.

"Too tired," replied Larry. "I'm going to catch up on my sleep."

Considering he wasn't even up when I left for school that morning, I didn't know when he could have got behind on his sleep, but of course I couldn't say that out loud.

"You should get a bigger tractor, Dad," said Nick, "like that one we saw last week. Then you'd never have to work after supper."

"Sure I would, Nick," said Dad. "I'd have to farm in the evenings because I'd be pumping gas in Dudley all day to pay for the tractor. I may have to do that anyway, even without buying new equipment."

"But, Dad!" I protested. "You can't get a job. You have too much work to do already."

"With the price of wheat so low, I'm going to have to do something, that's for sure." Dad must have thought I looked worried because he set down his fork and smiled at me. "Don't worry, Marjie. We won't have to leave the farm. We'll find a way to stick it out."

As if leaving the farm would bother me.

Trevor suddenly looked up from his plate. "The Gellers are going to move into the Brooke house right away," he said. "Craig rode home on the bus today."

He did? I must have been so deep in my book I didn't notice the extra stop. Since Pam moved away, I hadn't had anyone to sit with on the bus, so I always read.

"The painting must be done at last," said Mum, pausing with her knife over Angie's sausage. "When I was fitting Anne for her dress, she was complaining about how long it was taking."

"I wish it had taken a year," I grumbled.

"Leaving the house empty wouldn't bring Pam back," said Dad as if I didn't already know. "You'll just have to find other friends."

"But there aren't any girls my age anywhere near us," I said. "Lisa lives on the other side of Dudley, and Cheryl's even farther away." I stabbed viciously at a dill pickle. "There are probably a dozen eleven-year-old girls on the same block in Vancouver where Pam lives, and she can visit anyone she wants every day."

"In that case," said Mum, "why does she write that she's lonely and wants to come back?"

"Because she misses me, of course," I answered almost patiently. "We are still best friends, you know, even if she lives half a country away."

"Watch that tone of voice, Marjorie Elizabeth," said Dad, "or you'll find yourself eating outside."

"I'm sorry," I mumbled, but I wasn't really sorry. What did they care about losing best friends? All they thought about was farming and sewing and bossing kids. They didn't mind living in the middle of nowhere doing nothing. Except work, of course. They both just loved to work.

"I heard there's been another chemical theft," said Dad, proving that he really didn't care about me. "A grain elevator at Fox Ridge was broken into last night."

Even I was a little bit interested in that. Fox Ridge was a tiny village not far from Dudley.

"Fox Ridge?" said Trevor with his mouth full. "We played baseball there."

"We won, too," said Nick. "At least I think we did."

"Who cares?" I demanded impatiently. "What matters is that there was a burglary practically next door. Dudley might be next."

"You needn't lose sleep over that," put in Larry. "There are dozens of towns in Saskatchewan, and these robberies seem to hit pretty much at random."

"A robbery in Dudley wouldn't scare me," I said scornfully. "It would be exciting!"

"Hey, Dad," exclaimed Nick. "If they put a policeman in every elevator every night, they'd catch the robbers for sure."

"They can't do that," I objected. "There aren't enough policemen."

"That's right, Marjie." I felt a glow inside as Dad agreed with me. "And they don't just break into elevators," he went on. "Other businesses sell farm chemicals, too."

"But they wouldn't have to watch the places that have already had robberies," said Nick.

"They might steal from some more than once," I suggested. "After all, the dealers must get new stock when the old stuff is stolen. Then the rustlers could just come and take it again. They'd already know how to get in."

"Ha!" snorted Trevor. "Shows how smart you are, Marj. Rustlers steal cattle, not weed spray."

"They are so rustlers, Mr. Know-it-all. I heard a man on the radio call them rustlers." Mum handed me the potatoes. I took some and passed them on. "And I don't think they're stealing weed spray right now anyway. It's probably grasshopper poison."

"That's enough, you two," said Dad. "If you have to argue, do it outside so the rest of us can enjoy our meal."

"But I'm right, aren't I, Dad? Haven't you finished spraying weeds?"

"Yes, you're right," agreed Dad. "We've sprayed most of the crops for grasshoppers, too, though I have to check the canola again. I'm expecting the hoppers to move over from that pasture of Jack Kingsley's now the grass is getting so dry."

"When I grow up I'm going to be a policeman," said Nick. "I'd catch the thieves right away."

"I bet I could catch them now," I said. "If only I could get to Fox Ridge." I looked hopefully at Dad.

He laughed. "Sorry, Marj, you'll have to find your clues on the radio or in the newspaper."

I probably could find out who did it if I had a chance. I'd read every mystery in the Dudley School library and even solved a mystery once. I'd found the teacher's day book when one of the boys hid it between the mats in the gym storage room. Of course, that time I'd seen the thief leaving the gym when he was supposed to be in class, and this time I knew absolutely nothing about the crime.

If only I could get to Fox Ridge. Maybe there would be a clue that the police wouldn't recognize. Mum would sure be surprised. Maybe I'd even get my name on the radio or in the newspaper. Should I tell them my name is Marjorie or Marjie?

"Marjorie." Mum's voice interrupted my thoughts. "Are you ready for dessert?" I shook my head and glanced down at my plate. It was empty. Had I finished without realizing it or had someone switched plates? Both Nick and Trevor were already digging into their bowls of fruit, and Larry and Dad were talking farming, as usual, and drinking tea, not that either of them would take my dinner anyway.

Mum was looking at me kind of strangely. "Do you want dessert?" she asked.

"Uh, yes, please," I said. Some detective I'd make. I couldn't even figure out where my meal went.

Later, as Mum and I cleared the table, I told her I was going to go for a bike ride.

"Good. It's a lovely evening," she said. "Just clean the kitchen first, please."

"What?" I exclaimed. "The whole kitchen? I'll never get done."

"Then you'll never go for a bike ride," said Mum heartlessly. "If you hurry, it won't take long. Just wash the dishes that don't fit in the dishwasher, wipe the counters and sweep the floor. And don't glare at me like that or you can dust and vacuum the living room, as well."

I slammed a bowl into the sink and didn't even look to see if it broke.

"Listen," said Mum, "as a member of this family, you're required to help around the house. You can't spend two months doing only what you want."

"But today was the last day of school," I protested. "Can't I have at least one day off?"

"How many days do I get off?" asked Mum. "Or your father?" She smiled and her voice softened. "Come on, it's not so bad. I did the dishes after lunch. All you have is from supper." She tried to hug me, but I stood stiff and stared at the frying pan on the counter, a black, greasy frying pan with bits of sausage glued to the bottom. She sighed and turned toward the door.

"You'll have lots of time to read or play, Marjie," she said. "I promise."

She went upstairs to sew and left me alone with a kitchen piled to the ceiling with pots and bowls and clutter. I could have pretended I was a detective searching for a golden toothpick lost among the dirty dishes, but it looked too hopeless. Instead, I was a rich lady whose servants all got mad and quit because she didn't pay them enough. As I scrubbed, I told myself I'd be much kinder to my new servants and pay them twice as much.

Afterward, I shoved my feet into an old pair of runners and went to sit on the back steps. Scratching absentmindedly behind Rodos' ears, I watched Trevor and Nick play soccer.

Sometimes I couldn't help being jealous of them. Everyone should be twins, especially me. Then I'd always have a friend who would never move away, unless we went together.

If we moved to a city, my twin sister and I would window-shop in the mall every day after school, ride our bikes to the library on Saturdays and have a sleepover every night. She would help me with science and social studies, and I would help her with math and language arts. And when there were thousands of dirty dishes, I would wash and she would dry.

It wasn't hard imagining a twin—Pam and I had just about been twins, except we only had sleepovers on weekends. And she had moved away without me.

I stood up and kicked at a grasshopper munching on a flower growing by the step. Then I wandered over to the truck by the shop. Angie was standing behind it placing pebbles in neat rows on the bumper.

"Peas," she explained as I squatted down beside her.

"Does Daddy like you cooking on his truck?" I asked. "You might scratch the bumper."

"It's not Daddy's truck," said Angie. "It's mine."

"What do you mean? You can't drive."

"It says so right there," said Angie. She pointed to the license plate.

"That doesn't say Angie; it says AHP 538. That's the license number."

"It says Angie." She stuck out her bottom lip and glared at me. "That's how Mummy writes my name."

I gave up. If she wanted to spell her name AHP 538, I couldn't stop her. As I stood up, Angie brushed the pebbles off the bumper.

"Push me on the swing, Marjie?"

I hesitated.

"Please," she begged.

"Oh, all right, but only for a little while."

Angie didn't know the meaning of "a little while."

"Push me again, Marjie," she said after I'd pushed her at least a hundred times.

"I'm too tired," I told her. "My arms will fall off."

"Push me again."

"Do you want a sister with no arms?" I asked. "Then I'd never be able to push you."

I left her kicking her legs wildly, trying to pump, and went to pick up my bike. Angie needed a twin, too.

# CHAPTER 2

I GOT ON MY BIKE AND RODE, NOT NOTICING WHERE, JUST AWAY. Away from housework, away from little kids, away from parents who were always busy, away from the farm I didn't want to live on.

Why did Mum and Dad want to be farmers anyway? Stuck out here, hardly ever doing anything fun or going anywhere interesting. Working, working, always working, and expecting me to work, too. Kids aren't supposed to work. Kids are supposed to have fun. I'll work when I get really old. And I'll work in a city in a big office building with air conditioning for hot days like this one, and I'll buy all my clothes in a store, and I'll only cook when I feel like it. The rest of the time, I'll eat things other people eat, like store-bought bread and cookies that come in packages.

As my front tire hit a stone and I almost fell over, I added one more thing to the list: I'll only ride on paved roads. Better yet, I'll have a car.

Then I looked up, and there was the old barn.

I hadn't planned to take the trail. It made almost a straight line between our farm and Pam's, but I hadn't been on it since she'd moved during the Easter break.

Just past the barn, I turned off the main trail and bumped along an overgrown path to the gravel pit. On the edge of the pit was a boulder where Pam and I often sat and talked. It used to be huge but seemed to shrink every year. When we'd first started coming here, it was well over our heads. Now it barely reached my shoulders.

I leaned my bike against the stone and scrambled to the top. It was rough and warm against my bare legs. The scab from a mosquito bite I'd scratched too much rubbed off one knee. I had nothing to wipe it with, so I watched the blood make a crooked path down my leg.

Sitting on the rock, I felt as if I could see the whole world. The land stretched endlessly out like a giant's patchwork quilt in splotches of greens and browns, with a splash of yellow here and there from flowering canola. There weren't many trees to see, just an occasional shelterbelt row dividing the fields like stitching.

It wasn't flat the way most people expect Saskatchewan to be. There were little hills and hollows everywhere.

On the horizon to the east, I could see the elevators of Dudley with the houses nestled below them.

And down a gentle slope, right in front of me, but the length of two fields away, was Pam's farm.

When her father had gone to British Columbia after Christmas, looking for a job and a place to live, Pam and I both hoped he'd come back to say he'd changed his mind.

He didn't.

When he came back, it was to pack their clothes and furniture into a rented moving van. One Saturday, the auctioneers came and the fields around the farm filled with half-ton trucks. When they drove away again, all that remained were the buildings, and they belonged to a man named Jack Kingsley.

Now as I watched, I could see a truck back up to the door of Pam's old house and men start unloading the Gellers' expensive new furniture.

Actually, I didn't know if it was expensive new furniture, but considering how Mrs. Geller dressed, it seemed the only kind she'd have. She'd told Mum they'd had interior decorators from the city looking at the house. They'd talked about adding windows and rearranging doorways but finally settled on painting the whole place dove gray, inside and out.

It sounded awful.

I was never likely to find out for sure, though, not as long as Craig Geller lived there. I hardly knew Craig. He was a year younger than me, just going into grade five. He was the pitcher on the baseball team and won trophies for most valuable player when he played hockey.

And me? Well, I'd consider taking up sports only if I'd read every book in the world and the piano needed tuning.

But now Craig was going to live just down the hill from us, and we'd ride on the same school bus every day.

*If* he rode the school bus, that is. Maybe he'd go to school in the morning with his father, the principal, and come home afterward with his mother, the French teacher.

I lay back on the stone and stared at the sky, bright blue and almost cloudless, though it must have been close to nine o'clock. With the shortest night of the year just days before, it would stay light for at least another hour.

"Hey, Margarine."

I sat up, startled.

Craig Geller was straddling his bike at the edge of the gravel pit, a hand over his eyes, shading them from the sun.

"Oh hi," I said, scrambling down from the rock.

"I thought you lived around here," said Craig. He dropped his bike and glanced around. "But I don't see any farms besides ours. Excuse me, I mean Jack Kingsley's."

"We live in the hollow over there," I said, pointing up the slope where an outside row of trees was all that was visible of our farm. "What do you mean, Kingsley's farm? I thought your family bought it from him."

"Nope," said Craig. He jammed his hands in the pockets of his cutoffs and glared down the hill. "Kingsley collects farms," he said. "We're just renting. What would we want to buy it for anyway? We don't need a bunch of dumpy old buildings."

I didn't think the buildings were dumpy when Pam lived there, no worse than ours anyway, but I didn't say anything.

"The guy's a jerk," Craig burst out. "He says I can't go anywhere on the farm except the house and about two centimeters around it. What's the good of living in the country if you have to stay inside all the time?"

"Not much, I guess." If I was Craig, I wouldn't mind staying in the house all the time. He probably had a computer and Nintendo and no brothers to bounce soccer balls off his head while he practiced piano.

And if I never went outside, I'd never have to weed the garden.

On the other hand, I didn't like people telling me what to do either, even if it was what I wanted to do in the first place.

I picked up my bike and wheeled it closer to Craig so he wouldn't have the sun in his eyes. Not too close, though. I didn't want to have to look up to him. I hate being shorter than someone a whole year younger than me.

"This isn't Kingsley's land, is it?" he asked suddenly.

"No. This is ours. The summer-fallow field over there is Kingsley's." I pointed to a bare field partway down the hill that stretched all the way to the Geller's house by the highway. "I think he owns the fields across the highway, too, and the ones to the west."

"And what about the road?" asked Craig. "Was I trespassing when I rode on it?"

"Trail," I corrected. "I guess you were, but Dad doesn't care."

"That must be your barn then?"

I followed his gaze. It was an old weather-beaten barn with half a dozen tiny windows marching along each side and a big sliding door at the south end. Any paint had long since worn off, leaving the boards gray and rough. Next to it were odd pieces of wood as gray as the barn, a pile of stones and discarded machinery parts. Parked nearby was a rusting half-ton truck with a broken windshield, no tires and a license plate from 1963.

"Yes," I said, "but Dad's going to tear it down someday."

"Maybe we could find buried treasure in it," suggested Craig, "or bones from an unsolved murder."

He dropped his bike. I followed him toward the barn. I was surprised to see a shiny metal padlock on the big wooden sliding door.

"Dad must be trying to keep teenagers out," I guessed. "They sometimes have parties in the gravel pit. He's probably afraid they'll step on a rusty nail and sue him."

"Or fall out of the loft and break their necks and both legs," suggested Craig cheerfully. "Let's go inside."

"Inside? How can we? The door's locked."

"There are windows."

"Yes," I said, "boarded over."

"Not all of them."

I checked one side. Most of the windows were boarded, but a couple contained glass as gray as the surrounding wood from the years of dirt layered on them. They were so small even Angie would have had trouble crawling through.

"Hey, Margarine," came Craig's voice from the other side of the barn, "here's one."

On the side of the barn closest to the trail, Craig was piling discarded fence posts and rocks under an empty window.

"Get some more junk over here," he ordered. "A bit higher and we'll be able to reach the window."

I was sure Craig could never crawl through the tiny frame. I liked the thought of seeing him stuck, though, so I tugged a half-buried post out of the ground and carried it over.

Craig had his own ideas.

"You can go first," he said when we'd agreed the pile was high enough.

"I don't mind if you do," I said.

"It's your barn," said Craig. "Though if you're scared . . ." he added.

"I'm not scared." I looked at the pile of junk and the window above it. Being small might be an advantage this time. I just wished I knew what was inside.

I glanced at Craig, then stepped toward the barn.

I climbed slowly, feeling each stone and pole move and settle as I put my weight on it. It was Mount Everest. The rope tying me to the climber ahead had broken, and now I was on my own, inching my way up the steep face of the dangerous peak, not knowing when my foot would slip or a rock would move, plunging me to certain death.

I braced one foot on a fence post, about an inch away from a rusty nail, and grabbed at the windowsill. It was dirty, but I couldn't feel any glass shards. Mountain climbers can't be too fussy.

I pulled till my head and arms were in the barn, my bare legs still dangling outside.

It was cool inside and musty with no trace of the animal smell I was used to from the barn at home. After the brightness outside, I couldn't see a thing.

I suddenly remembered Dad telling Pam and me that we weren't supposed to go in the barn. "It's not safe," he'd told us last summer. "It's full of rotting wood and rusty nails. Stay out of there."

But that was last summer, when I'd been a whole year younger.

"What's the holdup?" called Craig impatiently from behind me. "Chickening out?"

"Waiting for my eyes to adjust," I told him quickly. I could feel my heart thudding in my chest. Can eleven-year-olds have heart attacks? I should have taken a different direction out of the yard or, better yet, stayed home and read a book.

No! I wasn't the Marjorie who's the smallest kid in her class and scared of the dark. I was a mountain climber.

But mountain climbers don't need to worry about pitchforks or piles of rotting manure carelessly left under a window for someone to fall into.

I turned over and pulled myself up till I was sitting, then dragged one leg at a time through the hole. It was a tight squeeze, but I thought I'd done it till I heard a ripping sound and realized I'd torn my shorts.

At least I hadn't torn me as well.

I eased off the window ledge and let go. The drop was shorter than I expected, with no pitchforks, manure or bones to greet my landing.

I was in the manger of an empty box stall. Light filtered through cracks all over the barn, revealing the partitions on either side of me ending just above my head and an empty doorway at the other end of the stall.

I was still looking around when Craig dropped lightly down beside me. I don't know how he made it through the window. He hadn't even torn his pants. I measured the hole on my hip with my fingers and wondered what Mum would say.

"It's falling apart," said Craig as we stepped out into the alley. He pulled on the door of one of the stalls and a board came off in his hand. He tossed it on the floor. "Wonder why there's nothing in here," he said. "You'd think your dad would at least use it for storage."

"We've got lots of storage at home," I said. "There's the quonset and a couple of old—" I stopped. After glancing into several empty stalls, we had found one that was in use.

"Well, look at that," said Craig, peering over my shoulder at the piles of boxes filling what looked like the biggest stall in the barn. "So he does use it. What's in them, I wonder?"

"Chemicals," I replied, recognizing the labels. The floor of the stall was nearly covered with boxes piled half a dozen high.

"Chemicals! What kind of chemicals? You mean like nitro-glycerin or sulfuric acid?" Craig grabbed my arm and pulled me out of the stall.

"They're going to blow!" he exclaimed. "They were set by international terrorists to explode as the train picks up speed across the bridge." He threw himself on the floor behind the wall and clutched my ankle.

"Dive for cover," he warned. "The train's coming! If you go in there, there'll be nothing left but bird feed."

I pulled my leg free and, leaving him crouching behind the wall, went back into the stall.

"If this was explosive," I said, "it would blow up everything from here to Dudley. That wall wouldn't save you."

"Sure it would," protested Craig. "It's reinforced concrete disguised to look like rotting wood."

I tried not to grin as he joined me in the stall and started reading one of the labels. "Aw, look at this," he exclaimed, sounding disappointed. "It's just grasshopper poison."

"Of course," I said. "Do you think they put pictures of insects on boxes of explosives?"

Craig looked closely at one of the pictures, then pulled a stub of a pencil out of his pocket and drew a moustache on a grasshopper. "How's that?" he asked, adding a top hat and cane.

"Wonderful," I said. "Jiminy Cricket. Where are his shoes?"

"More important," said Craig, shoving the pencil back in his pocket, "where is the door to the loft?"

"I don't know," I admitted. I looked up at the ceiling. "Our barn at home has a hole over each manger to throw hay down,"

I said, "but this one doesn't. There's probably a ladder by the door."

"You mean you've never been in the loft!" exclaimed Craig. "I'd have a clubhouse up there. It'd be the perfect place."

"Girls don't need clubhouses," I told him quickly, leading the way toward the big south doors. No way was I admitting we weren't even supposed to be in there.

Just as I'd guessed, there were boards nailed across the studs to make a ladder to the loft. While Craig was scrambling up, I noticed a dirty cap on the floor. I recognized it and tossed it out the window to take home to Dad. Then I followed Craig up into the loft.

We searched the whole barn without finding a single bone or hint of forgotten treasure. By this time, it was getting too dark inside to see.

Back outside I watched Craig ride down the hill on his bike, remembering all the times Pam and I had said good-bye at just that spot.

Then I picked up Dad's hat, climbed on my bike and started for home.

It was always a little harder going home because it was uphill. This time it seemed worse than usual as I hurried to beat the approaching darkness.

Remembering the noise I'd heard the night before didn't make me any braver. I looked around. It had come from this direction, but I really didn't think it was as far away as the highway.

Then into the stillness of the night, right behind me, came the lonely howl of a coyote. Another joined the first and then another till the night was filled with their mournful cries.

I wasn't scared. They were smaller than me. They didn't often chase people anyway. Especially someone on a bike. I was perfectly safe. I knew it. And if I said it often enough, I might even believe it.

Rodos bounded toward me, barking loudly as I rode into the yard. I stopped to talk to him, but he ran on past, barking at the coyotes. I barked once or twice, too, just to help Rodos out a bit.

It was good to be back home, where the lights in the house were bright and Mum and Dad were talking in the kitchen.

The howls of the coyotes faded away till the only place I could hear them was in my memory.

# CHAPTER 3

I SLEPT LATE THE NEXT MORNING TO CELEBRATE THE FIRST DAY OF summer holidays. When I came down for breakfast, Larry was still eating. Dad always got up early and was having his midmorning coffee.

I opened the fridge door, wondering what to eat, until an item on the radio drove muffins and cheese right out of my mind.

"There's been another break-in at a Saskatchewan grain elevator," said the announcer. Dad reached over and turned the volume up. "An elevator in the village of Dudley was broken into last night." I squealed and Dad motioned me to be quiet. "Unofficial estimates suggest between three and four thousand dollars worth of chemicals were taken in this latest incident.

"In the weather, it will be hot today, with moderate wind and no precipitation expected."

"Daddy!" I yelled as he turned the radio down again. "I told you they were going to rob Dudley next."

"There've sure been a lot of thefts this year," said Mum as she gave me a slice of toast.

"What would anyone do with that much spray?" I asked.

"Kill grasshoppers," said Dad.

"But not thousands and thousands of dollars worth," I objected, "unless each theft is by a different farmer."

"Are there that many desperate farmers?" asked Larry.

"More," said Dad. "But I don't think they are all out at night creeping into chemical sheds. The thieves probably sell most of the chemicals."

"Who to? Who's going to buy stolen spray? Wouldn't people tell the police?" Larry asked.

"Not everyone thinks like that," said Dad. "Besides, they might not know it was stolen." He stood up, pulling on his cap. "Most people would be happy to buy cheap chemicals," he added.

"I haven't heard anyone turn down a chance to save money yet," said Larry. He swallowed the last of his coffee and stacked the cup with his cereal bowl and plate.

"How much does a pail of spray cost?" I asked, following them outside into the sunshine and the heat. The gravel of the driveway bit into my bare feet. I hopped on my toes, trying to land between the pebbles.

"Depends on what's in it," Dad said. "Hair spray, now—"

"Doesn't come in a pail," I interrupted.

"Neither do most pesticides," said Dad. "They put it in jugs or cylinders now. Each costs a different price depending on the size and kind."

"Just an average," I persisted.

Dad sighed. "Maybe a hundred dollars," he suggested finally.

"A hundred dollars! For one container? And some cost more?"

"That's right," said Dad. "And some cost less."

"Boy, you must spend a fortune on chemicals every year." I tried to decide how many boxes we'd seen in the barn and multiply it by one hundred dollars.

"Not as much as I should," he said. "While you grease up, I'll check these bearings."

"I don't know how—" I began, then realized he was talking to Larry. Dad disappeared around the other side of the tractor, so I wandered back to the house. As I walked, a grasshopper flew up, hitting me on the lip. Realizing how close I'd come to grasshopper for breakfast, I decided to keep my mouth closed whenever I was outside.

The almost dark house felt cool. Mum had pulled the blinds to keep out the sun and was washing the kitchen table.

"You didn't eat your toast," she said.

I'd forgotten all about it. I didn't feel hungry but stuck it in the microwave for a few seconds anyway.

"Who do you think is stealing the chemicals?" I asked while I waited.

"Somebody too lazy to work for his money."

"Robbing elevators all over the province must take work," I objected. "They'd have to case them out ahead of time, then be sure no one saw them break in, then find someone to buy the stuff afterward."

"That's not what I call work," said Mum. She rinsed the dishcloth under the tap and started wiping the toaster.

"It would be exciting."

"So are some honest jobs. You could try vacuuming your bedroom, for instance."

"That's not exciting."

"Depends on what's under your bed!"

"Ugh."

I wanted to go for a bike ride. I'd take a book along and read somewhere out of reach of Mum calling me to work, but there was no reason to tell her that.

Mum hung her dishcloth on the rack and turned to look at me. "I want you to help till noon. Then you can do what you like while Angie's napping. I really have to sew more, or I'll never get done."

I thumped my glass down on the table.

"Marjorie!" said Mum sharply. "You know why I sew."

Drought. Low prices. If she didn't sew, I couldn't take piano lessons and I wouldn't have any clothes that weren't bought at a rummage sale and we'd probably eat wieners and beans every day. I'd heard it all before.

"I hate cleaning!" I replied and cut my toast into tiny little pieces.

"And I love it?"

"You get to sew."

"You'd like to take over? Perhaps you'll start with Mrs. Geller's dress. Of course, if you make any mistakes you'll have to replace the material, but it shouldn't cost more than fifty dollars."

Fifty dollars. Half a container of grasshopper spray. More money than I would have if I saved every cent I got for months. How many bushels of wheat?

"Why does everything cost so much?"

I didn't realize I'd said the words out loud until Mum answered.

"I don't know," she said quietly, coming over and putting her arms around my shoulders. "I just don't know."

I leaned against her for a moment. "Can you pay me to clean?" I asked, certain she'd say no and almost hoping she would so I'd have something else to complain about. Mum sighed and moved away. "I'll give you a dollar for working till noon."

A dollar for almost two hours work!

Oh well. It was better than working two hours for nothing, which was what I'd get if I protested. I poured a glass of milk and started eating my cold, hard toast, one tiny square at a time.

After lunch I read to Angie. I didn't mind. Her books are fun. But by the time I'd read *The Monster Under the Bed* three times, I was glad her eyes closed and her curly head flopped over on the pillow.

A few minutes later, I was on the trail, heading in the direction of the old barn. Grasshoppers buzzed by on every side of me, occasionally hitting my bare legs or arms with a thud and a sickening scramble of scratchy legs. The heat wrapped around me like a blanket, and I wondered if it would ever rain again.

I saw Craig's bike right away, leaning against the padlocked door. As I drew closer, I could see Craig himself sprawled on the grass nearby, staring at the ground.

"Hi, Margarine!" he called, jumping up. "I was hoping you'd come."

"My name is Mar-jor-ie," I said, pronouncing it very carefully. "What were you looking at?"

"Just some ants," said Craig. "Did you hear about the Dudley break-in? The police car just went by on its way to town," he said after I nodded. "Do you want to go see if they know anything?"

In the books I read, the police wouldn't be coming in the afternoon for a theft that had happened the night before, but Dudley was too small to have its own detachment. The RCMP came from Haley, an hour's drive away. From what I'd heard, they were never in a hurry. Imagine someone catching the thieves in the act of stealing chemicals and having to say, "Just sit down and wait, guys. The police will be here tomorrow afternoon."

Even slow police were better than none at all, though, so it wasn't likely I'd pass up a chance to see them working on a real mystery. "Sure," I told Craig. "But I have to be home when Angie wakes up about four."

"No problem," said Craig, glancing at his watch. "We've got loads of time. I'll just stop and tell Mum."

I waited outside while he ran into the dove gray house. I wondered if I should call my mother, too, but decided not to bother. It would just interrupt her sewing.

Craig came running back with a couple of juice boxes and

handed me one. It felt so cold I wanted to drink it right away, but I knew I'd need it more after we rode for a while. I tucked it into the waist of my shorts, where it immediately froze my stomach. Then I pedaled after Craig. His bike was bigger than mine, so I was afraid he'd get ahead of me. It didn't work that way.

"See that eagle up there?" he asked, stopping to point to a small, dark dot circling in the sky over the field.

"An eagle?" I said doubtfully. "I thought they lived in the mountains."

"Some do," said Craig, "and some don't."

As we watched, the eagle dove to the ground, then soared up again carrying what may have been a small rabbit.

I was watching the bird so closely I didn't even notice Craig watching me till he spoke. "Haven't you seen an eagle before?"

"I don't know. I don't notice birds much," I admitted. "Except owls. I like owls."

"You don't notice birds!" exclaimed Craig, in the same voice he'd have used if I admitted to stealing from the Dudley elevator. The rest of the way to town, he pointed out every bird he saw, telling me its name, life history and what it ate for breakfast. Fortunately, it was only five kilometers to town. We drank our juice halfway there. By the time we reached the road to the elevators I was already wishing for another.

It turned out we weren't the only ones interested in seeing the police investigate a real crime. The police car Craig had seen was parked by the elevator and so were about a dozen other vehicles and a bunch of kids on bikes. Craig immediately rode up to Tim and Aaron, boys from his class at school, and started talking. I hung back and wished we'd stayed home. I hadn't expected to find half of Dudley hanging around.

The door to the elevator opened and a policeman came out with a couple of other men.

The policeman looked bored as he glanced at the crowd

and then looked away. He probably solved so many mysteries it wasn't fun anymore.

One of the the other men opened the door to the chemical shed, they all peered in, then someone pushed it closed again. As they walked away, the door slowly swung open.

I watched the RCMP officer go back to his car. Then I got on my bike and, making a wide circle around the cars and people, rode behind the shed.

As soon as I got close to the shed, I noticed an odd, vaguely familiar smell. At first I thought it was from the village lagoon, which we can often smell if the wind is just right, but this was different, though just as awful.

Craig joined me a couple of minutes later. "Everyone's leaving," he reported. "Did you hear anything?"

"No. How about you?"

"I think they must have done all their talking inside the elevator," said Craig. "All I heard were complaints about the heat." He rubbed his nose. "What a horrible smell."

"They didn't even take fingerprints," I said.

"They may have before we got here," suggested Craig. "Not that it would do any good. The thieves would wear gloves anyway."

We wheeled our bikes around to the front of the shed. The only people left were two men in suits in a dark-colored car across the road. The back seat of the car was piled high with cardboard boxes.

"Let's look in the shed," suggested Craig. "The door's open, so no one will care."

We leaned our bikes against the wall and stepped inside. Craig pinched his nose. "The smell's worse in here," he said.

The shed was almost empty, with just a few boxes against one wall and a couple of jugs of 2,4-D near the door.

I pinched my nose, too. It shouldn't smell, I thought. The

chemicals should all be in sealed containers like the ones Dad buys. Then I noticed the pool of liquid on the floor by the boxes.

"It's leaking!" I exclaimed. "Look, Craig. The thieves must have dropped one, and it split open so they left it. Let's get out of here. That's poison!"

We turned to go, but it was too late.

The shed grew suddenly dark as a monster stepped into the doorway.

"Get out of here!" it yelled.

There was nothing I would have rather done, but the thing was filling the only exit. We hesitated a fraction of a second. It took a menacing step toward us.

I screamed and ran behind it out the door, Craig right behind me.

I might have run all the way home, but the monster spoke again and I glanced over my shoulder.

"This is a dangerous place," it said in an almost human voice.

It wasn't a monster at all. It was a man dressed in protective clothing and a face mask coming to clean up the spill. "What were you kids doing in there?" he asked, his voice muffled by the respirator. "Playing detective, I suppose?"

I looked at Craig. His face was flushed red with each freckle standing out brown. I'm sure mine looked the same, except I have fewer freckles. I took a deep breath and didn't even mind the man's scolding.

"Five more seconds and we'd have been as dead as the grasshoppers," said Craig when the man turned back to the shed. "Let's get out of here."

As we rode away, I noticed the man in the car was still watching us.

"Do you think they're the thieves?" I asked Craig. "Coming back to see if anyone suspects them?"

"Not likely," said Craig. "They're wearing suits."

"They're not glued on," I said impatiently. "They could have just put them on to throw people off the scent."

"Oh please," begged Craig. "Don't talk about scents right now."

As we rode past the other elevator, it seemed that many of the men had just moved down the road. "Got anything left that'll kill those hoppers in my canola?" I heard one of them ask. He was a short, stocky man. I couldn't see his face, but I thought it was Jack Kingsley, the man who'd bought Pam's farm.

"Not a thing," the elevator manager replied. "The truck should be in late tomorrow."

"Thanks, but if I wait that long, I'll be spraying an empty field."

"Good thing Dad has lots at home," I said as we left the elevator behind. "It sounds like there's a real shortage of chemicals right now."

"I wonder if the police will ever find the thieves," said Craig. "It didn't seem like they knew the first thing about looking for them."

"You never know. Someone might have been in town this morning doing the real investigation and he was just asking a few more questions." Too bad we hadn't been able to listen while they were in the office. If I was Nancy Drew, they would have asked for my help.

Craig didn't seem to want to talk on the way home, and I felt so hot and tired I didn't either, so we pedaled in thirsty silence. It was worse than riding camels in the desert. At least the camels would do the walking. I'd be free to watch for an oasis. I could see one just ahead of us with free pop and watermelon, but when we got close it dissolved into a herd of cows drinking out of a dugout. I wasn't that thirsty!

DAD DIDN'T COME IN FOR SUPPER. Mum said he was trying to get the spraying done while it was still calm.

"Where did he get the spray from?" asked Nick.

I opened my mouth to tell him where Dad was storing it, but took a bite of bread instead. I'd almost forgotten I wasn't supposed to go in the barn.

Mum answered. "He went to town today and got some from the other elevator," she said. "The thieves didn't break into both of them."

I spread a little more margarine on my bread and wondered why Mum thought Dad had bought spray when he had at least fifty boxes in the barn.

I looked at Mum, but she was eating as calmly as anyone can with Nick and Trevor wrestling and Angie complaining about the food. She obviously thought Dad really had bought the spray in town.

# CHAPTER 4

"THERE ARE MORE BOXES IN THE BARN," CRAIG WHISPERED INTO the telephone later that evening.

I yawned. "Yeah. So what?"

"So there was no chemical to buy in Dudley today, right?"

I stood up a little straighter and gripped the telephone a little tighter. "So maybe he went somewhere else and bought it."

"Why?"

"Why?" I repeated, stalling for time. "Because . . . because he needed a different kind, I guess."

"Marjorie," said Craig, "you know how many boxes were in there before?"

"Not exactly," I began.

Craig continued as if I hadn't spoken. "There are twenty-nine new boxes now, Marjorie. Twenty-nine. I counted them."

"Oh." There was nothing else to say. "I have to go Craig. I have to . . . I have to do the dishes."

I hung up the telephone and looked across at the sink, the empty sink, because I had already washed all the dishes, and Trevor and Nick had already dried them.

Twenty-nine more cases of chemicals, and Dad had sprayed today. I heard a truck drive into the yard. Dad must have finished.

I sat on the bench on the front step and watched him and Larry talking by the shop. Dad was wearing his dirty cap, the one

I'd found in the barn and hung in the porch. He didn't seem to have noticed it had been missing.

Dad glanced at his watch, accepted something from Larry that was too small for me to see and hurried to the house. Larry headed toward the bunkhouse.

"Hi, Dad," I said as he came up the steps, jangling keys in his pocket. "You missed supper."

Dad looked tired and dirty. "I'll miss more than that before this night's over," he said, hurrying past me into the house.

I talked to Rodos for a while before following Dad in.

"I didn't know you had a meeting tonight," Mum was saying as I came into the kitchen.

"Sorry, Carol," Dad replied. "I must have forgotten to tell you. I met Harvey in town this morning. He's called another emergency meeting to decide what to do about the water shortage."

"Oh, Ken, are you sure you have to go? You were up so early this morning."

"I'd rather not, but I said I'd be there." Dad unbuttoned his shirt as he talked. "Can you get me some clean clothes, Carol? I'm already late."

I sat down at the piano and played "Für Elise" over and over.

"Is that the only piece you know?" asked Dad a few minutes later as he came into the room, still combing his wet hair. Mum was sitting in her rocking chair sewing something no one in our family would wear. Dad bent over and kissed her cheek. "Don't wait up for me. This is apt to run late."

"Don't I know it," said Mum grumpily. "How many meetings is this business likely to take?"

Dad didn't answer.

I followed him into the porch. "Dad," I began.

He grabbed his cap, a clean, gray one, and turned to look at me. "Can it wait, Marjie? I'm already late."

What had I wanted to say anyway? "It's nothing, Dad," I said. "Just . . . good-bye." He smiled so briefly I almost missed it and then opened the door.

"Bye, Marjie girl. Be good." He ran lightly down the stairs and across the yard.

I watched the porch door swing shut behind him, then wandered back to the living room. I played "The Entertainer" this time, listening to Dad drive out of the yard. A minute or two later, there was the sound of another vehicle, and I knew Larry was gone, too.

I finished *The Mystery of the Moving Statue* and read most of *The Mystery of the Golden Ring* before my eyes started to shut all by themselves. Dad still wasn't in. I crept downstairs through the dark house. It was after midnight.

I opened the door and peeked outside. It was another warm, calm night, but it looked different from the other night. The yard light had been left on for Dad, and each building showed up clearly. Rodos heard the door open and came over to investigate. There were no strange noises, not even any coyotes, just the comforting croak of frogs out by from the dugout. I patted Rodos and went back to bed, yawning all the way.

Maybe there hadn't been any strange noises the other night either. Maybe I'd dreamed the whole thing. Maybe Mum was right, and I did read too many mysteries. Maybe there was a perfectly logical reason for having all those chemicals in the old barn.

IT WAS GETTING LIGHT outside when I woke again. A breeze was dancing with the curtains at my open window and blowing papers from the dresser to the floor. As I lowered the sash, I glanced around the yard. I could see Larry's car by the bunkhouse, but Dad's truck was nowhere to be seen.

I crawled back into bed and pulled the blanket up from

where it had fallen on the floor. Dad had been right. It was a very late meeting.

DESPITE THE LATE NIGHT, I woke up early to hear some birds having choir practice outside my window. Already I could hear the sound of a distant tractor. Was Dad out working already? Surely not after a night with almost no sleep.

"Good morning," said Mum, coming into the kitchen while I was digging in the drawer for a knife. "What are you doing up?"

I started spreading peanut butter on some buns. "I'm going for a bike ride," I explained.

Mum looked surprised. "At six in the morning?"

"It's cooler," I said, wondering what time Craig got up. Not at six, I was sure.

"At least you should get back in time to be of some use," said Mum. "Unless you're riding to Saskatoon today."

"Very funny." I didn't laugh. "Actually, I'm just going down the trail a ways." She looked as if she was going to ask another question, so I jumped in first. "Where's Dad?"

"Still in bed," she replied. "His meeting last night ran a bit later than usual."

"I know," I said, watching her face. "I woke up at dawn and the truck was still gone."

"That would be a very late meeting!"

I heaped jam on top of the peanut butter and squashed the tops of the buns on before dumping them into a plastic bag.

"Are you going to be warm enough in your shorts?" asked Mum.

I looked at her without saying anything.

"Okay, okay." She laughed and gave my shoulders a sort of hug. "I guess you won't freeze."

"Probably not," I agreed, slipping my bare feet into old canvas runners. "See you later."

I stepped outside and immediately wished I'd worn more

clothes. There was just enough breeze blowing to make goose bumps rise on my bare legs. It would get hot soon, though—it always did—so I let the door swing shut behind me and ran quickly down the steps.

A few minutes later, I leaned my bike against the barn and scrambled up the pile of junk to the open window. The first thing I touched when I grabbed the frame was the nail that had torn my shorts the other day. That pair was still on the floor in my bedroom, waiting for the right moment to show Mum. Not wanting to start a collection of holey clothes, I found a stone and hammered the nail in.

After dropping the stone back to the ground, I leaned against the rough wall of the barn and looked around. A gopher ran down the trail just in front of me. Another popped out of its hole and scolded noisily. Must be a mother gopher, I thought, and sighed. And what about the first gopher? It had stopped to chew on a stem of wheat. A father gopher, I decided, out stealing breakfast for his family.

I hadn't crawled out of bed this early in the morning to watch gophers, though. I had something to do.

It had seemed like a really good idea when I woke up. Go to the barn alone, look at the boxes, see for myself what they were. Maybe seeing them would tell me why they were there.

Now, standing on that pile of junk and shivering in the cool morning breeze, it didn't seem nearly so logical or so urgent. I considered going back home to bed. Instead, I turned around, grabbed the windowsill and pulled myself up.

The barn was dark and cool, but at least there wasn't any wind. I stepped gingerly down from the manger. It was more shadowy than I remembered.

I crept toward the door of the stall, then peeked around the corner. I couldn't see anything that hadn't been there the other day. I stepped out into the alley and headed for the stall full of boxes.

There was a faint scratching sound from the next stall. I froze in midstep, my heart pounding so loudly I could hear it.

A tiny shadow darted out of the doorway and ran in front of me.

I jumped, then leaned against the wall, willing my heart to slow down. It was just a mouse, and I certainly wasn't scared of mice.

Then I heard a noise that wasn't a mouse.

A scrambling sound, a thud, then footsteps.

I flattened myself against the wall and edged toward the opening in the next stall. Just one more step and—

"Hey, Margarine," said Craig. "What are you doing? Holding up the wall?"

"I was . . . waiting for you," I lied quickly.

I hoped my voice didn't show how scared I'd been. It was stupid to be scared, anyway. Who else was going to come into the barn through a window?

"And don't call me that horrible name," I said.

Craig looked surprised, and I knew I'd sounded more angry than I meant to.

"Sure," he said, "if I remember."

We walked in silence to the stall where we'd seen the chemicals.

"Rats!" said Craig.

There was nothing left in the stall but an abandoned mouse nest in the corner.

# CHAPTER 5

C RAIG AND I WALKED SLOWLY THROUGH THE BARN, CHECKING EACH stall, almost as if we expected to find the boxes moved to another spot. We didn't find anything. Nothing to suggest why the chemicals had been there . . . or why they were gone.

Finally, we climbed out the window again and walked around the outside of the barn. A patch of weeds by the door looked flattened, but the ground was too dry and hard to leave a tire track.

"We should have staked it out last night," exclaimed Craig suddenly. "I should have known they wouldn't stay here long." He dropped to the ground beside the barn, out of the wind.

"What do you mean?" I demanded, coming to stand in front of him. "You should have known who wouldn't stay long?"

"Not who," said Craig. "What. The chemicals. It's obvious. No one's making any money while the chemicals sit here, so they have to get them out and sell them."

I felt as if my stomach had dropped to my feet, and something, maybe my heart, was plugging my throat so I couldn't talk. Finally, I squeezed the words out, my voice sounding strange even to my own ears. "What are you talking about, Craig? Who has to sell the chemicals?"

"The thieves, of course," said Craig, looking excited. And why wouldn't he? It wasn't his father's barn. "They have to be

47

stolen, don't you think?" he went on eagerly. "You told me your father never keeps anything in here. And twenty-nine boxes showed up right after there was a robbery in Dudley.

"It's the ideal place for a thieves' hideaway. Out of sight of our place . . . your farm . . . barely visible from the highway. Now we just have to figure out who the thieves are and catch them."

"You . . ." it came out as a squeak, so I cleared my throat and tried again. "You don't have any ideas, do you?"

"Not yet," said Craig. "Say, you don't happen to have any food with you, do you? I'm starving."

"Oh. Oh yeah." I remembered the breakfast I'd packed for myself. It seemed like a lifetime ago. "Sure, I'll get it."

I brought the bag from my bike and offered Craig one of the buns, thinking furiously the whole time.

"What I can't figure out," said Craig when he'd finished a bun in about three bites and asked for another, "is how they have a key to the barn."

I looked at the shiny padlock on the weather-beaten door. I remembered when Angie took the candy from the grocery store. Dad made her give it back and apologize even though she was only two at the time.

"Maybe the thieves put the padlock on the door," I suggested, "because they didn't want someone going in there and finding the chemicals."

"But it's so bright," argued Craig. "Your parents would notice it."

The padlock hanging on the dingy, gray door of the old barn shone in the early morning sun. I went over and tugged it. The metal felt warm in my hands. "Maybe I was right before," I said slowly. "Maybe Dad did put a padlock on the door just to keep teenagers out. And then . . ." I paused and Craig jumped to his feet, finishing the sentence for me.

"And then the thieves cut it off and put one of their own on, so if your father ever tried to get in, it wouldn't work and he'd just think he had the wrong key."

I sat down and leaned against the barn. It was possible, but it didn't explain where Dad got the spray yesterday, and it sure didn't explain why he went to a meeting on a night he didn't usually have meetings and stayed out so late.

"What did you think of those men at the elevator yesterday?" Craig asked.

"The ones in the car full of boxes? Well, they sure were interested in what was going on, but if they were the thieves, how would they know about this barn? It's not on a road where people usually drive. Hardly anyone uses this trail."

A grasshopper jumped onto my leg, and I flicked it off. It hit the ground and hopped away. I hoped it had a headache.

"What are you doing up so early?" I asked Craig after a long pause.

"I always get up early," he said, dropping down beside me. "Sometimes I go birding, or Dad and I go fishing, or if the weather is lousy I just read. It was bad when we lived in Regina because I was stuck in the city unless Dad or Mum took me somewhere."

"I'd love to live in a city."

"I don't like towns," said Craig, "not even little ones like Dudley. Houses all around and cars driving by when we're trying to play road hockey and dogs barking all the time. Not that this is much better when I'm not allowed anywhere on the farm except the house and a yard the size of a piece of computer paper."

"Then your father should have bought the yard," I suggested. He has lots of money, doesn't he?

"What would we do with a barn, a chicken house and a bunch of granaries? Can you see my mother gathering eggs?"

I couldn't.

"Oh well. At least we're not in Regina anymore."

"That's where I want to live," I said dreamily. "A city. A library with a million books. I wouldn't have to request books and wait weeks for them to come. They'd be right there, and I could go every day if I wanted, not just twice a week. And the stores—"

"And the noise and so many people and pollution and the smells from the industrial area and the crime."

"We have crime," I reminded Craig. "And pigs. They smell."

"They're your pigs," said Craig. "And the smell won't give you cancer. We lived on a corner lot, and a car drove over our lawn at least once a month."

"That happened to someone in Dudley once, too."

"See, that's why you live on a farm."

"But farmers don't have any money," I protested. "Dad gets up at six almost every day of his life." Except today! "And it's not because he likes mornings and wants to go bird-watching. He works till dark or later almost every night. When I need something, he tells me we can't afford it because the price of wheat is dropping and the price of fuel is going up."

Craig didn't say anything for a moment, just dusted the crumbs off his lap. We both watched while an ant came and carried a crumb away.

"That's why Pam moved to B.C., isn't it?"

I nodded, blinking rapidly so the tears wouldn't come. "They live in Vancouver now. She hates it there."

"What'd I tell you? Cities are the pits."

"If we lived in the city, Dad would work just eight hours a day and we'd have lots of money and Mum would have time—" I stopped talking and jumped to my feet. "Let's ride over to McCroskeys' and see if their horses are near the fence. They have the most beautiful Paint I've ever seen."

I jumped on my bike and tore off down the trail without

waiting to see if Craig was behind me. What did he want to hear about farming for? When my parents were working their hardest, his had the whole summer off. And while my parents were telling me they didn't have enough money to buy new pencil crayons for school, he had his own computer.

"We're not the only ones up early," said Craig when he caught up to me. "See Kingsley out there?" I followed his pointing finger to a tractor in the field across the highway from Craig's house. "Isn't it too windy for spraying?"

I pushed back a strand of hair that was blowing in my face. "I would think so," I said slowly. "Craig . . . where did he get his spray from? He was the guy in town yesterday asking for some, and they didn't have any."

"Yeah," said Craig. He looked thoughtful. "He was."

We watched McCroskeys' horses for a while, but I hardly even thought about what it would be like to own one, the way I usually did. I was too busy thinking of people who managed to spray without buying chemicals.

Mum didn't look too pleased when I got back to the house. "There you are at last," she said, her hands sticky with bread dough. "I thought you were going for an early ride so you'd have more time to help."

"I met Craig and we rode over to the McCroskey's."

"What on earth for?" Without waiting for an answer, she went on. "Go help Angie get dressed, will you? Last time I saw her, she was putting on her white dress. When I told her to change, she burst into tears."

She wasn't crying when I found her, but she hadn't changed either.

"Hey, little Angelkin," I said, "if you wear that around the house you'll get it stained."

"It's pretty," said Angie, putting down her red crayon and picking up a blue.

"It is pretty," I agreed, "and we want to keep it that way." She looked absolutely adorable in the frilly dress with the little pink roses dotted all over it. Mum did make nice clothes, not that she had much time to make them for her own family. She was always sewing for someone else. People who paid.

I finally bribed Angie to change by reading her two stories and coloring a page in her book. By the time we went back to the kitchen, she was wearing shorts and a T-shirt and the shortest ponytail I'd ever seen.

"Isn't she beautiful?" I asked Mum. She looked up from scraping the bread dough off the table and smiled. "You're both beautiful," she said. "Or you would be if you combed your hair."

I ran to the bathroom mirror. My hair looked worse than usual but no wonder with the wind out there.

Mum kept me busy with one job after another all morning, and I really tried to work hard, but my thoughts kept interrupting me.

When it was time for lunch, Angie was nowhere to be seen. I checked the playhouse, the strawberry patch and the sandbox. Then I started looking around the out buildings. Eventually, I found her by the bunkhouse arranging pebbles on the bumper of Larry's car. It was a sporty, red car with bucket seats in the front and hardly any room in the back. I wasn't sure how he'd like her playing on it. He was very careful to keep it clean. A scratch would probably kill him.

"What are you doing here?" I asked Angie, scooping her up for a hug.

"Put me down, put me down," she squealed. "I'm making dinner."

I flopped down on the ground to watch her. "What are you making?" I asked.

"Carrots and sketti," said Angie. "Want some?"

"I'm not really hungry right now, but thanks anyway." I

leaned against the car and watched her. I sniffed. There was a faint, unpleasant smell that I couldn't quite place.

I stood up and wandered around the car. The keys were dangling from the ignition. An idea occurred to me.

"Oh, my goodness," I exclaimed. "It's dinnertime, Angie. That's why I came to get you."

"Carrots and sketti?" she asked hopefully.

"Almost," I said. "It's macaroni and cheese."

She brushed her pebbles onto the ground, and I swung her up in the air. We ran to the house with Angie giggling louder at every bouncing step.

I was in luck. Larry had taken a lunch with him when he went summer-fallowing, and Dad drove away as soon as he'd eaten. I only had to read Angie two books before she snuggled into her pillow. When I came downstairs, the boys were snapping each other with tea towels and they'd hardly started on the dishes. I had the yard to myself.

I went straight to the bunkhouse. Sure, the boys would be able to see me if they looked out the kitchen window, but that wasn't likely.

The driver's door of Larry's car was on the side away from the house, so I opened it. The handle was hot, but the keys were worse. There were just three on the ring, the big one I'd pulled out of the ignition, a smaller one that was probably for the trunk and a tiny one.

I left the door ajar, darted around to the back of the car and fumbled with the key in the trunk. I tried the middle-sized one first, then the small one, then realized I'd had the right key first but had held it upside down.

The smell grew stronger as I lifted the lid of the trunk.

I'm not sure what I'd expected to find, but it wasn't there. All the trunk contained was a red, metal toolbox, the spare tire, and a small container of something that was leaking from the lid. The label was covered with the dark liquid that had leaked out. I reached in and turned the container over. I had just barely made out a picture of a car when I heard a vehicle drive into the yard.

I'd been holding the trunk just partway open. Now I slammed it shut and dropped to my stomach behind the car. Between the wheels of Larry's car, I saw black tires roll by. It was the old green half-ton that Larry used around the farm. It stopped in front of the shop, and Larry climbed out. He disappeared into the shop, probably to get a tool to repair something out in the field. I pulled the keys out of the trunk lock, got up on my knees and started crawling around the car, checking constantly to see if he was coming back out.

He hadn't appeared by the time I reached the driver's door. I reached in, dropped the keys on the seat and gently pushed the door shut. It wasn't quite flush, but it would do till he was gone. If only he hadn't noticed it open when he drove past.

I crawled backward to the rear of the car, then peeked underneath. Larry was coming toward the car.

There was only one place I could go without being seen.

Fortunately, there were more weeds than gravel under the car. I slithered quickly under just as Larry reached the driver's door. He opened it but didn't get in. I heard the jingle of keys and some other noise I couldn't identify. I prayed he wouldn't decide to move the car. A moment later, Larry slammed the door shut and walked back to the truck. I stayed where I was until the truck was out of the yard.

Back in the sunshine, I saw what Larry had stopped for. He'd opened the windows on the car to let the heat escape. The keys weren't on the seat where I'd left them, but I wasn't surprised. He'd needed them to open the power windows. But they weren't in the ignition either.

He'd taken them away.

"You can finish the dishes for us," said Trevor when I went back in the house.

"You wish," I said. I poured myself a glass of ice water and plopped down on the piano bench. I hadn't even grown tired of practicing scales when the telephone rang.

"I found something," said Craig. "It's important."

"What is it?"

"I can't tell you over the telephone. Can you meet me at the barn in ten minutes?"

"In this heat?"

"I thought you wanted to solve this."

"But they're gone now. Isn't it too late?"

"I told you," Craig was back to whispering, "there's been a new development."

"Must you whisper?" I demanded. "I can't hear a word you're saying."

"The walls have ears," Craig whispered a little louder. "See you in fifteen minutes."

# CHAPTER 6

I WENT UP TO TELL MUM I WAS GOING.

"Take my watch," she told me, slipping it off her wrist. "And come back in an hour. Angie will be awake by then. If I can sew till supper, I should be able to finish this." She slid a piece of flowered fabric under the pressure foot of the sewing machine and stepped on the pedal.

Craig was pacing up and down in front of the barn when I rode up. "You're late," he called, running to meet me.

"What's the development?" I asked. "Find a suspicious foot-print?"

"Better than that," said Craig, grabbing the handlebars of my bike and practically pulling it out from under me. "I found a marked chemical box."

"Marked?" I said, letting the bike drop. "Marked with what?"

"A moustache, a cane and a hat," said Craig.

"What are you talking about?"

"You remember," said Craig, brushing a grasshopper off his leg, "the first time we were in the barn, I drew on one of the cartons of Warrior."

"And now you found it? Where?"

"In Kingsley's garbage dump."

I let out a long breath. "Wow!"

It was behind the granaries, south of the yard.

"Mr. Kingsley started spraying early today," I said. "The

thieves hardly had time to sell the chemicals to him by six this morning."

I stopped. There was another possibility. "Unless," I said, "unless Mr. Kingsley is the thief."

"That's why he's spraying today even though it's windy," exclaimed Craig. "He's trying to get rid of the evidence."

"Except he didn't. He just dumped the boxes in his yard."

"He doesn't know one of them was marked."

"It was your doodling, was it?" I asked. "I mean, Mr. Kingsley didn't just draw pictures on the box, and you thought it was yours?"

Craig gave me a disgusted look.

"So Jack Kingsley is definitely involved," I said. I took a deep breath and smiled at Craig. If Jack Kingsley was the thief, then it didn't matter how late Dad stayed out at meetings.

"Either he stole them, or he bought the chemicals from the real thief."

I sighed. "Then we still don't know anything for sure?"

"Sure," said Craig. "We know that one of the boxes was thrown away in Kingsley's junkyard. Do you want to phone the police or shall I?"

I cleared my throat. "The police?"

"Yeah, you know, the people who catch thieves and put them in jail."

"We don't even have any stolen chemicals to show them."

"But we have the box."

"But what if the thieves did see your doodles and threw it out of the truck and Mr. Kingsley . . . Mr. Kingsley found it and put it in his dumpyard because he . . ."

"Doesn't like littering?" finished Craig.

I turned my head and studied the summer fallow. There was a patch of volunteer grain coming up near the trail. I looked at it for a long time. Of course we should call the police, I thought. There were stolen chemicals here, they're gone and we find a marked box. The police talk to Kingsley. He says he . . . What does he say? He found it? He never saw it? He bought it from someone?

My stomach felt suddenly sick. I sank down to the ground, then looked up to see Craig's eyes on me.

Finally, he spoke. "Why don't we wait till they put some more in?" he suggested.

"Okay," I agreed willingly. Any delay was good.

"Too bad I hadn't doodled on more of them," mused Craig. "When the next shipment arrives, we can mark every box."

"Next shipment? Maybe they're done now."

"Not likely," said Craig. He tried to step on a grasshopper, but it hopped away. "And while the stuff is here, we should use some on these hoppers. They're really starting to bug me."

"And they're not even eating your crops." I glanced at Mum's watch. It was time to go. "You know what I'd really like to do? I'd like to change the padlock on that door. Then no one could put any more stolen chemicals in there."

"That would just put them on their guard, and we'd never find out who they are."

"I'm not sure I want to," I said. "I just want them to stop storing chemicals in my dad's barn. They can put them any-where else they like, just not here."

MUM WAS SMILING WHEN I GOT HOME. The dress was going faster than she expected. "I think I'll start on something for you next week," she said. "I want to get it done before the garden comes in, or I won't have time. Speaking of garden," she added, looking at me sideways, "wouldn't you enjoy hoeing a few rows this afternoon?"

"Mum!" I cried. "In this heat?"

"Well, if you can ride a bike in it . . . Never mind, maybe we can all go out this evening, when it's a bit cooler." She started the sewing machine, and I turned to go but stopped when she spoke again. "Where did you ride today?"

"I met Craig," I said, after a long pause that made her look at me curiously. "We didn't ride anywhere. We just sat and talked. He doesn't like grasshoppers."

"Who does?" said Mum. "You should invite Craig here sometime. He might like to play with Nick and Trevor."

"Mum!" I exclaimed, horrified. "He's three years older than they are. He wouldn't want to play with them."

Mum shrugged her shoulders. "Then he can play with you. I'm sure it would be a nice change for him. He doesn't have any brothers or sisters. It must be very quiet around his house."

I looked around Mum's bedroom. The window was the old-fashioned kind that lifted up and down. The ledge was stained dark brown from moisture. There were cracks in the plaster of the ceiling and water marks where rain had leaked in. They were old stains. It hadn't rained yet this summer.

And the downstairs was worse. The furniture in the living room was frayed, the wallpaper was peeling off the kitchen wall and there was a hole in the flooring by the sink. What would Craig think of a house like this? How could I possibly invite him over?

So I didn't. But Craig asked me if I'd go bird-watching with him the next morning.

FOR SOMEONE who couldn't stand sitting around, I was surprised at how still and quiet he could be while we watched the red-winged blackbirds and meadowlarks. I tried to be still, too, but it was difficult with swarms of mosquitoes acting like we were an unexpected breakfast treat. I'd hardly seen a mosquito all summer because it was so dry. They were still around the water, though, and it seemed that every one of them found me.

Afterward, Craig invited me to his house for breakfast. On the way through our yard, I waved to Dad, who was kneeling in the driveway by the shop, changing cultivator shovels. Larry was helping him.

The dove gray house wasn't boring. To be honest, I kind of liked it. It was lighter inside than when Pam had lived there. It wasn't all one color either. The kitchen had white cupboards now, and the ceramic apples on the windowsill matched the bright red potholders and the placemats where Mrs. Geller set our heaping plates of bacon and pancakes. I was glad she left us alone after pouring the orange juice.

After I'd eaten more bacon than Mum would have approved of, we went to Craig's room and played computer games for a while. As we passed through the living room, I saw blue furniture and a patterned carpet that wasn't quite big enough, so the wooden floors showed around the edges. There wasn't a paper or toy in sight. If the windows and doors hadn't been in the same places, I would have thought they'd thrown out Pam's house and started fresh.

That afternoon, it was too hot to be outside, and I hadn't been to the library to get any more books. I played the piano for a while, then wandered upstairs thinking about that letter to Pam I hadn't finished. I couldn't find the one I'd started, so I tore a blank sheet of paper from one of my old notebooks and found a pen under my bed but didn't know what to say.

After staring at the empty page for a long time, I finally told Pam that Craig had moved to the farm and called me Margarine, and Mum made me work all day so she wouldn't have to, and the twins were building a fort in the trees right where we'd had one two years ago.

THE FIRST OF JULY fell on a Sunday, so Dad came on the Canada Day picnic, too. Larry had left after supper on Saturday, planning to be back early Monday. Trevor and Nick thought this would mean more food for them, but they didn't complain a bit when Mum told me to invite Craig, even though I was sure he'd eat more than Larry. His family had relatives visiting, but the only kid was a baby, so Craig was glad to get away.

Instead of going to the park, where everybody else goes, we had our picnic in a place where the lake followed a coulee into a pasture and formed a finger of water. Dad liked to fish there once or twice a year. The water was so low that it made a great swimming spot and left lots of shore to play on. Dad said our swimming chased away the fish, but I think it was just too shallow for them. I doubt he cared anyway. He didn't like eating fish; he just wanted to sit and hold the fishing rod and look like he was doing something when, for once, he really wasn't.

Trevor and Nick had brought along their soccer ball, and we all played. Well, almost all. It was me and Nick and Mum against Trevor and Craig, with Angie getting in our way and kicking the ball any old place.

I was surprised when Dad said he didn't want to play; he usually likes to. I tried to make him change his mind, but he sounded pretty grouchy when he answered. Then Mum called me over to help her get some stuff from the car. When we were out of sight, she told me to leave Dad alone. She said he had a few problems right now, and he just needed a little space.

We had a fun game anyway, and I almost forgot to wonder why Dad didn't want to play. We only quit when Mum said her legs were too tired to hold her up anymore. She said it was supper time anyway, so we all roasted wieners and ate macaroni salad and vegetables and dip and fresh cherries. When we were as full as we could be, Mum brought out the Canada Day cake I had made, and we ate most of that, too.

It was a wonderful day, even if we didn't catch any fish.

The next morning, there were thirty-seven boxes of chemicals in the barn.

# CHAPTER 7

ICOULDN'T GET TO SLEEP THAT NIGHT. I GAVE UP TRYING AFTER A WHILE and re-read a book I'd gotten for my birthday. It wasn't as exciting when I already knew what was going to happen. I dozed off in chapter eight. Later, I woke up and crawled out of bed to turn off the light.

A warm breeze stirred the curtains. I leaned against the window for a moment and smelled the freshness of the night. My eyes were drawn to the black shape that was Rodos. He ran across the yard and into a shadow near the shop. After a moment, I realized someone was standing in the darkness.

It was getting closer to dawn. Even in the few minutes I stood at the window, it got lighter outside so I could tell who was standing beside Rodos, his hand resting on the dog's head. When I finally crawled, yawning, back into bed, Dad was still standing in the shadow by the shop.

I arrived in the kitchen for breakfast just in time to hear the lady on the news dash my hopes that the whole thing would go away. She reported two chemical thefts in the town of Robinson.

"Where's that?" I asked Dad when he and Larry came in for coffee. Hearing the report didn't seem to bother him, but I hadn't expected it would. When we play games in the winter, I never get hints about Dad's cards by looking at his face.

"North and east, I think," he said. "I'm not sure. Why don't you look on a map?"

I found a road map of Saskatchewan and brought it back to the kitchen. Robinson was in the east all right and a long way from Dudley. Would the thieves store the chemicals this far from where they'd taken them?

When I told Dad where Robinson was, he just grunted and poured himself more coffee.

When Craig phoned later that morning, I learned that, yes, burglars do hide things that far from where they take them.

The next time I heard the news on the radio, the announcer added that police were asking for public assistance in finding the chemical rustlers. People could report anything suspicious and remain anonymous by calling the Crime Stoppers Hotline. I turned off the radio before he said the number.

I was tidying the living room when I heard a vehicle drive into the yard. Glancing out the window, I saw Jack Kingsley get out of his truck.

"What's he doing here?" I asked Mum, who was down on her knees sorting through Angie's toy box for lost socks.

"Who?" she asked without looking up. I told her.

"Oh, he probably wants to borrow something or just talk. How should I know?"

I decided the window facing the shop needed cleaning and got the bottle of spray and some rags. Dad and Mr. Kingsley leaned against the red truck talking for about fifteen minutes. The inside of the window got very clean, but I could only guess why he'd come. Some of my guesses were the kind I didn't want to think about. When he drove away without borrowing so much as a hammer, I liked them even less.

"Aren't you going to do the other one?" Mum asked. "It's just as spotty."

"Another day," I said.

I didn't see Craig's bike when I got to the barn after lunch, but he popped out from behind the old truck and beckoned me. "Hide your bike here," he said, "so no one driving by will see it."

"What's the problem?" I asked, obediently wheeling my bike around to the patch of weeds where Craig had put his. "You know no one uses this trail but us."

"And Jack Kingsley," said Craig. "I saw him go right by here this morning."

"He and Dad talked for a while. I didn't know he came this way, though."

"Did you hear what they talked about?"

I shook my head.

Craig looked at me, frowning slightly. He opened his mouth to speak, but I jumped in first. "Come on. Let's go mark those boxes."

I took six steps before Craig moved. "Yeah," he said. "Sure." He ran past me and scrambled up the pile of junk first. Grabbing the window frame, he walked straight up the side of the barn. No wonder he got in so quickly. I gingerly climbed the pile, which seemed to be getting shorter each time as the junk settled, then pulled myself up to the window. If I did that regularly, I'd get terrific arm muscles.

Thirty-seven boxes looked like a lot of chemicals. I sank down onto one of them and leaned against the stack, my eyes closed. If I was really lucky, maybe they'd disappear before I opened them again.

I felt something hit my leg and fumbled for the black marker Craig tossed me.

"Here, get busy," he said.

I watched him draw a moustache on a grasshopper.

"I don't think that's a very good idea," I said, studying his artwork. "It looks good, but they're going to wonder how all the grasshoppers suddenly sprouted mustaches."

Craig looked at the box regretfully. "Then what? They should be marked."

"How about just a few lines in some obscure spot," I suggested. "Or even just coloring in the o's on the back of the box.

"I suppose so."

I could tell Craig really wanted to draw more hats and canes, but he had to agree with me. We decided to color in the o's in the line that said "Directions for Use." With just the two circles to fill in, it didn't take long and would be noticeable only to us. We had to move some of the boxes but made sure they all went back where we'd found them, except for the box of Warrior with the hairy grasshopper. I hid that one behind a couple others.

Afterward, Craig got out a notebook and recorded how many boxes of each kind of chemical there were. They weren't all grasshopper spray this time. There were some weed killers and even some for drying the leaves of crops to make harvesting easier. It looked as though chemical rustling could go on till winter. There was always something new to steal.

"So what time do you want to watch tonight?" asked Craig when we'd finished the count.

"I'd sort of planned to sleep tonight," I hedged.

"Go to bed early and sleep then," suggested Craig. "How many hours of darkness are there?" He didn't give me a chance to answer. "It's not likely the burglars are going to do anything around the barn much before midnight. Too much chance of someone coming by and seeing them. It starts to get light by five o'clock in the morning, so we only need to watch for . . . Let's see, even if we started watching at eleven, that would be only three hours each."

"Where do we watch from?" I asked, trying not to show my nervousness.

Craig glanced around. "Not in here," he said to my relief. "If we could see them, they would probably see us, too. How about the clump of trees over by the gravel pit?"

"Then we couldn't see the door," I reminded him. "How about that old truck on the other side of the barn? It's close enough to the barn so we'd be able hear if anyone speaks. We could hide underneath it."

"Okay," said Craig. "We'd be close enough to slash their tires if we want to."

"I thought we were just trying to find out who it is," I said, "not warn them that someone is watching."

"Keep your shirt on, Butterface. It was just an idea."

"What did you call me?" I interrupted. "Craig the Egg. Or maybe—"

"It's just a joke," interrupted Craig. "Don't get so upset."

"If you don't want me to get upset, try calling me by my own name." I turned and headed out the door.

"Hey, wait," Craig called after me. "We still have to decide when we're going to watch the barn."

I looked at him over my shoulder. Waiting.

"Oh, come on, Marjorie. Don't get mad."

"Say it again."

"Marjorie," said Craig. He grinned. "Sounds an awful lot like—"

I took two steps out of the stall. "Aw, Marjorie, I was kidding. Honest. Do you want first shift or second?"

Did I want to get up at eleven or two? I didn't know how I could get up at either time. It would be dark. There might be coyotes. Could I take Rodos along? No. He wouldn't lie still if someone drove up to the barn, especially someone he knew.

I came back to Craig. "You know," I said, "we could lie out there and freeze all night, and maybe nothing will happen."

"Yeah," he said. "And we could go home and be warm, and all these chemicals could disappear, or someone else will find out they're here, and whose barn is this?"

"What do you mean?"

"Just what I said. Think I don't know why you didn't want to call the police?"

"My dad's not a thief," I glared at Craig. He didn't exactly glare back, but he looked stubborn.

"Well, then, let's call the police. If you're sure it's not your dad, there's no problem."

I looked at the floor, the same floor where I'd found Dad's cap the first time we'd come into the barn.

There was a long silence.

"It's not that cold out," said Craig at last, just as if we'd come to some kind of agreement.

"All right. I wish I had an alarm clock, though. I'm afraid I won't wake up."

"I'll lend you mine. I'll bring it over later."

"How about if I come now and get it?" I suggested. Craig still hadn't been in our house, and I intended to keep it that way, if I could. Nick and Trevor had had such a good time playing soccer with him yesterday that they were already talking about another game. "Mum doesn't like us borrowing things," I said, "so I'll have to smuggle it in when she's not around."

"Sure," said Craig. "Guess we're done here anyway." He jammed his notebook and the markers back into his pocket and headed for the window.

I WAITED OUTSIDE Craig's house while he went inside for the alarm clock. After handing me the brown paper bag, he invited me in for a game of Monopoly.

"I'd better not," I said. "Mum will be expecting me to watch Angie."

"Do you take care of her every day?" asked Craig.

"I guess so," I shrugged. "Mum is busy with her sewing so somebody has to make sure Angie doesn't stand behind a tractor."

"I wish I had a sister," said Craig enviously. "You're lucky. And you've got brothers, too. That was great yesterday. I sure couldn't see my mother joining in a game of soccer."

"Well," I said uncomfortably, "Mum doesn't do it often either."

"I guess she's busy most of the time."

"Yeah, that's right," I agreed. "Well, I better go. Thanks for the alarm clock. I'll take good care of it."

"Don't worry," said Craig. "I have two."

I picked up my bike, then remembered our stakeout. "How about if you take the first shift?" I suggested. "I'll be out there by two unless it rains." I squinted up at the sky—blue and cloudless. It was bright enough to make my eyes hurt. "I'll be out there by two."

# CHAPTER 8

IT WAS A CLOCK RADIO, SO THERE WOULDN'T BE A LOUD ALARM TO wake Mum and Dad at one-thirty in the morning. Of course, there might be only Mum to wake.

All I had to think about now was setting the clock so it was loud enough to wake me and not loud enough to alert the rest of the house. I hid it under my pillow in case someone came into my room, then went to bed early.

I hadn't realized how noisy our house could be in the evening. Usually I go to bed after Angie, and Trevor and Nick, but tonight they were free to run up and down the stairs, yell and beat on the walls. I wanted to tell them to be quiet but was afraid of the questions I'd face if Mum learned I was trying to sleep at eight-thirty in the evening.

It wasn't just the kids that kept me awake either. I had never staked out a building before, but I'd read enough mysteries to be afraid.

What if someone saw us? What if we saw someone we knew? I'd heard on the radio that there had been forty-eight chemical thefts this year. If they stole two thousand dollars worth each time, that would be almost a hundred thousand dollars. And they probably took more. Thirty-seven cases would cost much more than two thousand dollars.

If a thief found someone spying on him, what would he do? Is a hundred thousand dollars enough to make someone violent? How long would a thief who's robbed forty-eight chemical dealers stay in jail?

My bed grew hotter with every moment. I turned the pillow a dozen times, looking for a cool spot that wasn't there. Whenever I checked Craig's clock, certain that half an hour had passed, it was never more than five minutes.

There were twelve thieves, and they were all strong enough to carry three boxes of chemicals at a time. They had seen the doodles on the box of Warrior and were looking all around the barn. They noticed the pile of junk under the open window and were just checking beneath the old truck when . . .

I woke up. It was one o'clock. I was sweating and cold at the same time.

That's enough. Any more dreams and I'd never have the courage to leave my room, let alone ride in the darkness all the way to the old barn.

I dressed quickly in a dark jogging suit and crept down the hall. Halfway down the stairs, I remembered the alarm clock and went to turn it off. This time I thought of bringing a blanket to put on the ground, but the one on my bed was pink. I left it there and decided to borrow the navy-colored one Mum kept in the car.

I crept back down the stairs, freezing against the wall every time a step creaked. I heard someone snoring and wondered who it was. Mum says Dad snores; Dad says it's Mum. I wanted to check but didn't dare. It sounded like a male snore anyway, which meant Dad was at home in bed, where he belonged.

I grabbed a handful of cookies as I passed through the kitchen, then left the porch door unlocked behind me. There was nothing in our house valuable enough to steal.

I fed Rodos two cookies, then left two more on the step to keep him occupied till I was gone. I wished I could take him with me, but he probably wouldn't have come anyway. He hardly ever leaves the yard.

The yard light was off, but the moon shone so brightly I didn't miss it. There were shadows everywhere. One was certain to be hiding something terrifying. My heart thudded heavily in my chest, and I felt cold, though I knew the night was warm.

How did I get myself into this? I didn't want to catch the burglars. I wanted them to go away and leave us alone.

I jumped on my bike and rode quickly away while Rodos crunched his cookies. The blanket was wrapped around my waist like a very thick belt. It slipped off a couple times, and I had to stop and wrap it around again.

I was surrounded by quiet. No coyotes. No strange noises. No vehicles or slamming doors. Just crickets and frogs and, once, an owl.

Did that shadow move? There was a light breeze. Maybe it was just a swaying branch.

No, something was moving across the trail. There were no trees near enough to cast a shadow, and it wasn't my imagination. I dropped my feet to the ground, wondering why it wasn't still last week when I stayed at home reading books and the most important thing in my life was the sadness about Pam moving.

The shadow turned into a cat. It slipped across the trail and disappeared into the wheat field on the right.

I started riding again. There was nothing here that wasn't also here in the daylight, I told myself. I just couldn't see it so well in the dark.

I looked straight down the trail and kept riding, praying all the way that I was right.

There were no extra vehicles or signs of movement at the barn, so I took my bike around to the back and laid it among the junk, where I hoped it wouldn't be noticed should anyone come. Then I tiptoed toward the truck. I tripped over a piece of metal hidden in the grass and fell forward. Something moved beneath my foot, and I grabbed the truck box for support.

"Ow," said Craig. "Can't you watch where you're going?"

"Sorry," I said, trying not to laugh. "I thought you were going to hide under the truck."

"No room," said Craig. "That truck's been here so long, it's part of the prairie."

"I hope no one will see us out here," I said, not feeling good about watching from an exposed spot, even if we were on the far side of the truck from the barn. "Has anything happened?" I asked, though I had already guessed the answer.

"Nothing but a few new mosquito bites and a bad case of boredom. The thieves must be smarter than us tonight. They're home in their beds."

"You were the one who wanted to stake out the barn."

"I still do," said Craig, interrupting himself to yawn, "but it's just more exciting when something happens."

"Maybe they were just waiting till I got here," I suggested. The thought terrified me. What if they did come? What was I supposed to do?

"If they come," said Craig, reading my mind, "you won't be able to do much." He sounded regretful. I cheered silently. "But you can try to get their license number and descriptions of the people and the vehicles. You can use my notebook if you didn't bring one."

"Of course I did," I said, "and a pen." I'd zipped both into the nylon fanny pack I got for my birthday.

After assuring himself that I wouldn't ruin his investigation if the thieves happened to arrive, Craig rolled up his sleeping bag and slipped into the shadows. In the stillness of the night, I could hear his bike for a couple minutes after he left. If we rode up while the thieves were there, they would hear us coming. I made a note on the first page of my book to mention this to Craig tomorrow. I couldn't see what I'd written, so I turned the page, ready to put my next note where it wouldn't land on top of the words I'd already written.

Listening while I lay in the shadows was a bit like being blind. Would blind people be afraid of the dark? If they were, they would be afraid all the time.

Just a couple of days ago, I wanted to move off the farm more than anything, but then I expected Dad to come, too. He was supposed to get a job and earn lots of money so we could buy new clothes and a food processor and take summer holidays.

If he was in jail, we would have to move where no one knew us, and Mum would work twelve hours a day in a restaurant to feed us. Then she'd sew all night to pay the rent, and I'd have to make all the meals, except when Mum brought home leftovers from the restaurant.

I'd probably have to quit school in grade eight to join Mum at the restaurant, and Trevor and Nick would make the meals. The first week we would all get sick from their cooking, and the second week we'd die. Dad would get out of jail after fifteen years and find his family all dead. He would be so sad he would rob another elevator, so they'd put him back in jail, where he'd waste away and die of a broken heart.

It started to get light sooner than I thought it should. I sat up with a start and realized I'd been sleeping. Well, if a truck had come, I would have woken up, so I guess it didn't matter. But I wouldn't tell Craig. The sun was just barely showing over the fields in the east. They weren't likely to come now, not when people could see them.

I bundled up my blanket, climbed sleepily onto my bike and rode home. Rodos was sleepy, too. He looked up when I rode into the yard, saw it was just me and settled back down. I crept into the house, locked the door and snuck up to my room. I think I fell asleep before I even got into bed.

THE NEXT EVENING, I helped Mum weed the garden. Nick and Trevor were supposed to be helping, too, though they spent more time eating strawberries and chasing each other with over-grown pigweeds. By the time I'd had my bath, it was dark outside and Dad had come in. I dressed in the dark jogging suit again and waited for Mum and Dad to go to sleep so I could slip outside to cover the first shift. I had nothing to read, so I cleaned under my bed while I waited.

Mum had been wrong. It wasn't exciting. I did find a moldy orange peel, though, and an overdue library book.

I could still hear voices from Mum and Dad's room, but Craig's clock warned me that if I didn't get going I'd be late. I gathered up a bundle of junk from under the bed in case Mum heard me and wanted to know why I was up, and crept out of the room. The voices were louder in the hall. I stopped outside their closed door.

Mum sounded angry. "I'm sick of all this," she said. "I never see you anymore."

"It's not going to be this busy forever. A few more weeks . . ." Dad's voice trailed off.

"A few weeks! You know it'll be more than that. And Larry's worse than no help at all."

I didn't want to hear anymore. I wasn't as quiet as I should have been going down the stairs, but no one besides me seemed to hear the creaks. I dumped the papers in the wastebasket in the porch, grabbed some cookies and stepped outside.

Rodos seemed to be waiting. I'd have to make some more cookies tomorrow, or I wouldn't have anything to bribe him with.

It was dark outside, but the moon was bright and I had a lot on my mind. I rode all the way to the barn with hardly a thought about what might be in the dark with me.

I stayed brave right up to the moment I cuddled in my blanket beside the truck and the coyotes started to howl.

# CHAPTER 9

I COULD HEAR RODOS BARKING AT THE COYOTES, HIS VOICE SOUNDING small and far away. The coyotes sounded close, too close.

It wasn't just one coyote. There must have been a whole pack of them. Looking for food. With Rodos guarding our yard, they wouldn't kill our chickens, but he was too far away to protect me. I lay and shivered and worried and prayed, but the coyotes didn't stop howling.

There was a rustle in the weeds. I peered into the darkness, seeing nothing but shadows. Then I saw an animal standing on a rise on the far side of the gravel pit, a silhouette against the night sky. It howled a long, mournful cry.

I needed a dog, so I pretended I was one—a big, black dog with a deep voice. I barked.

There was a pause in the howling. I barked again, the best imitation of Rodos I'd ever done. I heard him answering from the yard. The coyote on the hill disappeared. Then more appeared and disappeared. They were moving away from me down the other side of the hill. When they howled again, it was from a long way off.

I managed to stay awake during my watch this time. If it was from fear of the coyotes, I might as well have slept. They didn't return and neither did the thieves.

"Good," said Craig when he came to relieve me. "Then they'll come while I'm watching."

If they were going to return at all—and with thirty-seven cases of chemicals waiting for them they probably were—I hoped it was while Craig was there.

I sped home, looking forward to bed too much to worry more than briefly about what was lurking in the dark. As I glided into the yard, I found something new to fear.

Dad's truck had been parked beside the gas tanks when I left. I remembered it distinctly because I'd had to swerve around it as I rode out of the yard. When I got back, it wasn't there.

Sure it was dark in the yard, but not dark enough to hide a half-ton. I stopped my bike right where the truck had been three hours before. I could see the shadow of Mum's car by the house, Larry's car nearby, beside the bunkhouse, and the grain truck over by the granaries. There were a couple of tractors in the yard, too, and the shadow of the old green truck Larry used to haul fuel to the tractors. Nowhere in the yard was Dad's light blue half-ton.

I gave Rodos a half-hearted pat and went up to bed. I could hear the snores, but this time I knew they were Mum's. It seemed women could snore after all.

It was a long time before I went to sleep.

When I got up, the truck was back beside the fuel pumps, and Dad and Larry were working in the shop.

The theft in Tritton was the first item on the news when I went downstairs, so I was prepared for Craig's excitement.

"I saw them," he exclaimed when we met at the barn after lunch. "There were two men in a light-colored half-ton."

I felt pain and looked down to see my fingernails digging into the palms of my hands.

According to Craig, the two men were an average size and wearing dark coveralls. The truck was parked at an angle to the barn door, so he wasn't able to see the license plate from his hiding place.

As the men unloaded from the back of the truck, Craig had crawled up to the front. This time he couldn't read the numbers on the license plate because they were coated in dried mud. He wanted to scratch it off but was afraid they'd hear the noise or finish unloading before he was done.

"The mud must have been put there intentionally," finished Craig. "It hasn't rained in weeks."

"C–c–could you see them by the interior light when they got in and out of the truck?" I asked.

Craig bent down and pulled a blade of grass. He started picking off the crisp, brown edges. "I didn't look," he admitted at last. "I thought they'd see me by the light from the truck, so I stayed out of sight till they closed the doors.

"I have to find a new suspect," said Craig after a long silence. "You know what Jack Kingsley looks like?"

"Yeah," I said. "Short, stocky."

"Fat," said Craig. "Neither of these guys was fat. One was a bit taller than the other, but they were . . . normal sized." There was an awkward silence.

"We did think there could be more than one thief," I reminded Craig. "Maybe there are several, and they take turns." I wanted Jack Kingsley to be the thief. It wouldn't wreck my life if he went to jail.

"Did you hear them talk?"

"Not clearly," said Craig. "I could hear some mumbles while they were in the barn, and one of them said something while they were closing the barn door, but it made so much noise I couldn't make out what he said."

We climbed through the window and marked the newest boxes—all twenty-two of them.

MUM WAS WEEDING the flower bed by the porch door when I got home.

"Did you get tired of sewing?" I asked, kneeling down beside her.

"You could say that," she replied. "I've finished everything I started. I do have some jogging suits to make for Connie Graham, but I decided to leave them till tomorrow."

I flicked away a grasshopper that was chewing on a flower.

"I think I'll just finish these flower beds this afternoon," Mum went on. "It's not nearly as hot today as it's been the last while. Maybe it'll work itself up to rain yet."

"I thought heat was supposed to bring rain."

"Sometimes it does, but it hasn't this summer, so maybe the cooler weather will."

"Would the rain kill the grasshoppers?"

"Not when they're adult. It'll keep them from eating while its raining, though, and the plants will get stronger and be able to take it better." She pulled some tiny weeds from the base of a flower. "And it will cheer your father."

"Does he need cheering?"

"How would you feel if you were watching everything you worked for fry in the field?"

"Not very good, I guess. Are there grasshoppers in Vancouver?"

"Why don't you ask Pam?"

"Why don't we move there, too? Dad could get a job in the same place as Mr. Brooke, and he wouldn't care about the weather."

"Your father is a farmer," Mum replied. "It's the only life he wants. You know he can't stand being in the city for more than a couple of days."

"But it would be better," I protested. "There's more to do there."

"If we went to the city, we'd be broker than we are now and probably less contented, too. Wouldn't you miss your bike rides?"

I turned away to pull some weeds beside me, hoping I didn't look as guilty as I felt. Here Mum thought I rode my bike for hours everyday, and I'd mostly been riding only as far as the barn.

"I could ride in the city."

"With traffic zipping by?"

I wasn't used to traffic. There wouldn't be as many birds to watch either. With Craig talking about birds so much, I'd found out they were more interesting than I'd ever thought.

Rodos came and stuck his head under my arm for a hug. "And what would we do with him?" asked Mum. "He's too big to live in town."

"But you wouldn't be so busy and neither would Dad."

"How do you figure that? We'd probably each have to have two jobs to make ends meet." She sat back on her heels and looked at me soberly. "Honey, moving away wouldn't solve all our problems. People take themselves with them wherever they go. And people make their own happiness."

I kept pulling weeds.

"Do you think you're unhappy now?" she asked.

"Of course," I started to say. But then I stopped. Sure, I missed Pam, but I liked Craig. It was different having a boy for a friend. Even our search for the chemical rustlers could be fun, if only I wasn't so afraid of the answer.

# CHAPTER 10

I WAS GOING TO STAY AWAKE UNTIL IT WAS TIME TO GO TO THE BARN again, but my eyes had plans of their own. Giving in, I set Craig's clock for ten-thirty and stuffed it back under the pillow.

I woke later to a still, silent house and knew I'd overslept. After a frantic search, I found the radio unplugged on the floor. Hoping it hadn't been damaged in the fall, I swept it quickly under the knot of blankets on the bed.

If it was cooler during the day, it was apt to be cooler at night, too, so I put on sweat pants under my jeans and a bunny hug on top.

The clock in the kitchen said twelve-thirty when I crept past. The thieves had come later than that the other night. I could only hope they'd do the same tonight.

Rodos met me at the door, but before I gave him the cookies, I looked around for Dad's truck. Though it was darker than I'd expected, I could just make out the truck beside the shop. Rodos got an extra big hug with his cookies. Then I was on my bike, heading straight out of the yard.

It was colder than the other nights, and the wind was picking up. Going with it now, I was grateful for the extra layer of clothes. Coming home would be no fun.

It must have clouded over since sunset because there weren't any stars. I longed to be snuggled in my bed listening to the wind whistling through the trees instead of feeling it whistle through me.

The barn was dark and silent. I stowed my bike in the pile of junk and wrapped myself in the blanket before dropping down behind the truck. The wind hit me square in the face when I lifted my head, so I pulled up the hood of my bunny hug and lay flat.

As I lay there shivering, it suddenly occurred to me that the thieves might have already come. If they'd already added a new shipment of chemicals to the barn, I might as well go home where it was warm.

I felt under the truck for the flashlight Craig said he would leave there, hoping I wouldn't pick up a snake by mistake or be bitten by a mouse. Fortunately, all my hand touched was dry grass before I felt the smooth roundness of the flashlight. I was getting much better at doing things I didn't want to do.

I flicked it on to make sure it worked, then immediately turned it off again. Did I dare climb into the barn alone? It would be dark in there. Pitch dark. It was dark enough outside tonight.

I wouldn't have to stay long. It would probably take less than five minutes to go in, see if anyone had been there and come back out. I stood up and dropped the blanket to the ground.

The cold snaked under my sweater. How could it be so cold after all the heat we'd had? I felt my way to the front of the truck, where there was less junk to trip over. From there, it was just a couple of steps to the barn.

The wind pressed me against the roughness of the wall. My hand moved along it, lightly guiding me to the corner, then to the window.

The barn at night was not like the barn in the daytime. It was totally dark, totally mysterious. But I had the flashlight.

I was only going in so I wouldn't have to wonder for the rest of the night if I'd missed them. Right?

As soon as I was standing in the manger, I pulled the flashlight out of my waistband, where I'd stuffed it for the climb, and flicked it on. I panned it quickly around the barn. Everything looked reassuringly normal.

Jumping down lightly, I hurried out of the stall and down the alley to where the chemicals were kept. They were still there, the two shipments we had marked with darkened *o*'s, and nothing else. The thieves hadn't been there yet.

I had taken just one step out of the stall when I heard the truck pull up outside.

With the noise of the wind, I hadn't heard it approaching. There was no time to get out. I didn't dare head for the loft with the ladder right by the door. My legs were frozen in place, and all I could hear was my heart beating in my ears.

The jangle of someone unlocking the padlock cut through my fear. I darted quickly across the alley and into the opposite stall. They hadn't stored anything in other stalls before; I prayed they wouldn't tonight either. But they might check the barn first.

I pressed myself against the wall beside the door to the stall, hoping that even if someone looked in, he wouldn't see me.

Then the quiet was ripped by the sound of the door opening. Loud and long, it was even more scarry than the night Rodos and I had heard it from the safety of our porch step.

My straining ears picked up a rattle and bang as the thieves opened the tailgate of their truck, then footsteps as someone entered the barn.

They came closer, closer, then turned the other way and into the opposite stall. There was a small thump as a box was set down. Another thump followed quickly. There were at least two people.

The footsteps came and went, truck to stall, stall to truck. I counted ten trips. Now and then, there was a brief comment.

Once one of them swore. I guessed he'd dropped the box on his finger.

"Just one more," one of them said after the tenth trip. "I'll get it." A single set of footsteps walked to the door of the barn and back to the truck.

"That's it," he said, dropping the box with a thump.

"You're right. That's it," said a different voice, a familiar voice. "I've had it with this business. I dream about Mounties knocking on my door."

"Only one more night," said the other voice, so quietly I wouldn't have made out the words if they hadn't been standing on the other side of the wall from where I leaned in terror. "Tomorrow night we deliver this load and let him worry about it."

"Them maybe we'll get some sleep," said the other. He laughed softly, and they turned and walked out of the barn. In the silence following the screech of the closing door, I heard the padlock snap shut.

Fear forgotten, I left my hiding spot and made for the door at a run, hoping to catch a glimpse of them. I heard the tailgate slam and almost panicked. There was no moonlight streaming through to guide me to a crack. I felt with my hands, but it was useless. Finally, I thought of the edge of the door. Sure enough, part of it had broken away, leaving a crack.

The dark shadow of one man was just barely visible as he opened the door of the truck. I hoped to see him better in the glow from the interior light, but it didn't happen. The light didn't come on.

When the truck pulled away without headlights, I realized the lack of an interior light was no accident. These guys weren't taking any chances. How they could see was beyond me. I wondered what might have happened if they'd been a few minutes earlier and I'd still been on the trail.

As the truck drove away toward our farm, the sound of the motor was quickly lost in the whistle of the wind.

There was no hurry to leave the barn now. They wouldn't be back tonight.

I went to the stall with the window and stretched out in the manger. I was safe, but my heart was still beating like a metronome on prestissimo. I'd recognized one voice but not the other. And who was getting the chemicals tomorrow night? How many people were involved in this anyway?

After a while, there was a scrambling sound behind me.

"Marjorie?" Craig whispered. "Are you in here?"

"Right here, Craig." He dropped into the manger beside me. "They were already here," I said. "I heard their plans."

"You did?" said Craig. "Way t'go!"

I smiled, and I couldn't stop. It was a good thing it was dark.

As I told Craig what I'd heard, my heart slowed down to almost normal, and I started to think that maybe, just maybe, everything would work out yet.

Before we went home, we made our plans.

# CHAPTER 11

IT WAS CLOUDY AND COOL THE NEXT MORNING, A GOOD DAY FOR baking, Mum said. Dad was working in the shop when I brought him some warm cookies.

"Are you going to spray today?" I asked. "It's not windy."

"I'm not doing any more spraying," said Dad. "Not till fall anyway."

"Does that mean the grasshoppers are all gone?"

"No." Dad stopped filing the piece of metal he was holding and wiped his hands on a greasy rag. "It means it would cost more than it would be worth to do it again. The adults don't die as easily as the young ones, and when we drive on the crop this late, it gets damaged. In this cool weather, the grasshoppers aren't eating much anyway."

"Do you think it will rain?"

"Within the next year? Probably."

"Today?"

"You tell me." He was beginning to sound impatient, so I handed him another cookie.

"Marjie? Where are you?" Through the open double doors of the shop, I could see Angie running toward the barn.

"Trevor found the kittens," she shrieked. "There are five, and two are mine."

I followed her across the yard, past the half-ton. I noticed a row of pebbles on the bumper. Angie had been cooking again.

Right under the bumper was the license plate. It didn't spell Angie's name today. It didn't spell anything. It was coated with a thick layer of dried mud.

Angie tugged on my hand. "Come on," she urged. I took a bite out of the last cookie I had left and chewed thoughtfully. She pulled me past Larry's car. I glanced inside. The windows were closed again, and there was no sign of the keys in the ignition. I tried the door. It was locked.

Then I heard a sound behind me.

I swung around. Angie was watching me . . . and so was Larry. He'd come out of the bunkhouse and was standing on the step, looking right at me.

"What are you doing?" he asked.

"N–nothing," I said. "Do you want some breakfast? I'll tell Mum you're up."

"Sure, kid," said Larry. He didn't smile. "Where's your father?"

I told him, then ran to the house, certain I could feel Larry's eyes on my back the whole way.

The telephone rang just as I walked in the door. Craig wanted to start working on the barn this morning. With Mum working in the kitchen, I couldn't say much but okay. I hung up, told Mum Larry was coming in, then ran back out to see the kittens with Angie.

Twenty minutes later, I parked my bike out of sight of the trail and climbed inside the barn to help Craig mark the *o*'s on the new cases.

"We'll have to oil the door," said Craig. "They probably won't notice the difference when they open it, but it will make it easier to close."

"They can't get through the window," I said firmly.

"No," agreed Craig, "but we could nail boards over it anyway so they won't even think of it."

"We'll have to cover the entrance to the loft, too," I said, looking around the barn for possible escape routes. "If they got up there, they could jump out the loft doors."

"Hammers, nails, boards, oil," said Craig, penciling a list in his notebook. "Anything else we need?"

"Not that I can think of." There were no holes in the barn walls or the loft floor big enough for anyone to crawl through. Of course, if they were in there any length of time, they could make a hole, but I hoped it would take awhile if they didn't have tools.

We went outside, first checking to make sure no one was in sight. All we needed to wreck our plans completely was for anyone to see us hanging around the barn.

It was the door we inspected the most carefully. Craig grabbed the bottom of the door and tugged to see if it would come out of the metal channel it ran in. It moved a bit but didn't leave the channel.

"The wood is pretty rotten," I pointed out. "If two angry men are shoving on the door, they could push the door out far enough to escape."

"We could brace it with some of those old fence posts," suggested Craig. "It only has to last a couple of hours."

"You hope." I glanced far above my head at the top of the door. The glides were really rusty. "I'd feel better if we could try out the door," I admitted. "If we can't get that door closed and the padlock on it fast enough, those guys are going to catch us, and I don't want to be caught."

Then I had another thought. "What if they take the padlock off when they unlock the door? We won't be able to lock them back in."

"Good thought," said Craig, whipping out his notebook. "We'd better bring another padlock just in case."

We decided to come back after lunch, me with the hammer,

nails, padlock and oil, Craig with scraps of lumber from Kingsley's junkyard. Craig didn't appear to be taking Kingsley's restrictions too seriously.

Dad was still working in the shop when I got back to the yard. I wandered around, chatting about nothing in particular, noting where the oilcan and hammers were kept. The padlock was a little harder. I couldn't see one anywhere but knew there had to be one because Dad usually locked the fuel tanks with a padlock when we went away, not that that happened much.

"Aren't you supposed to be helping your mother?" Dad asked suddenly and unexpectedly.

"I don't know."

"Well, I do. Go inside and make yourself useful. You know she has more work than she can handle."

"Aye, aye, sir," I said quickly. I saluted and left the shop, almost tripping over Larry on my way out. He was lying on the ground half under the truck, but he rolled out as I passed him.

"Watch where you're going, eh?" he said. I shivered and not just because it was a cool day.

"It's about time you showed up," said Mum when I stepped into the kitchen. She looked up from piercing the crust of a pie. "I thought you were going to help me bake today."

"Oops!" I exclaimed. "I forgot."

"Either that or you just decided not to help." Mum set the pie on the oven rack beside two others and slammed the door shut. "Wash your hands and start putting the buns on the pans. And you can help after lunch, too, since you left without permission this morning."

"But, Mum . . ." I began.

"But nothing," she said. "Get busy with those buns."

I sighed and started shaping buns. I didn't know how I was going to do it, but I had to get away this afternoon. And I had to find a padlock.

"THERE'S THE KITCHEN TO TIDY," said Mum after lunch, "and the bathroom to clean. I'll set the timer for the last pan of buns."

"Can I go after I'm done those things?" I asked hopefully.

"Not today. You knew you were supposed to help this morning, and you left, so now you can stay here. You could practice piano for a while if you get your work done."

"But, Mum . . ."

"But nothing. I'm going upstairs to sew. Don't let the boys come trooping upstairs. I want Angie to sleep. She seemed a bit warm this morning. I hope she's not coming down with something."

"But, Mum . . ."

"Don't forget to make coffee for Dad and Larry at three-thirty. You can call me then, too."

"But, Mum . . ."

She was gone. I glanced at the clock. One-thirty. The buns wouldn't be out of the oven until almost two. By then I had to find a padlock, collect the oilcan and hammer and nails I'd hidden while Dad was in for lunch and do all the work Mum had left me. There was no way.

I heard the screen door slam behind me. "What are you doing, Marjie?" asked Nick, coming into the kitchen. "Want to come play with Trevor and me? We're—"

"No," I interrupted. "Mum gave me a pile of stuff to do. Hey, Nick, do you know where there's a padlock?"

"I've got one, but you can't have it."

"I don't want it. It's too small. I need a big one, like the one Dad uses when he locks the fuel tanks."

"He stores that one in a drawer out in the red tool chest in the shop," said Nick, "but that's the only one I know about. What do you want it for anyway?"

"Oh nothing," I said, taking the broom from behind the

door and starting to sweep the floor. "Can you help me clean the kitchen? Mum told me to do it, and I don't have time."

"Why don't you have time?" Nick reached into the cookie jar, then turned to look at me accusingly. "I bet you're going to see Craig again. That's not fair. I want to go, too."

"If you help me," I said slowly, "I'll let you come with me . . . tomorrow." That should work. Everything would be over tonight. "Mum says I can't go anywhere today."

"Promise I can go tomorrow?"

"Promise."

"What about Trevor?"

"Only if he helps, too."

The twins agreed to clean the kitchen in return for spending time with me and Craig the next day. I hoped Craig didn't have other plans, but I'd worry about that when tomorrow came. For now I was glad to leave them wiping the counters and washing the pots and bowls from lunch while I sponged out the bathroom sink and changed the towels.

"Take the buns out of the oven when the timer rings, and don't forget to turn off the oven," I instructed Nick as soon as I felt I could call the bathroom done. "I have to do something outside, but I'll come back as soon as I can."

"Wait," yelled Trevor. "Where are you going?"

"Don't yell," I said, pausing with my hand on the door, "you'll wake up Angie. I'm not going anywhere. I can't. Mum told me to stay home. I'm just going outside for a while. Don't tell anyone where I am."

As I ran out the door, I heard his voice calling behind, "How can I? I don't know where you're going."

Dad was out in the shop. Just my luck.

I walked in, trying to look as if I hadn't a thing on my mind and was just visiting. There was the red tool chest right over where Dad was working. I wandered around, looking at all the tools and piles of greasy stuff lying on the workbench. And there was another red tool chest. Which one had Nick been talking about?

I pulled open one of the drawers.

It squeaked and Dad glanced up. "Now don't go taking my tools and leaving them all over the yard."

"I won't, Dad," I said quickly. "I don't want any tools. I was just curious about what you keep in all the drawers."

"Go ahead and look. Then you'll know where to put things back if you ever borrow anything."

I looked in every drawer. No padlock. It must be in the one beside him, but if it was there, I couldn't take it without him seeing.

I went over to the other tool chest, just inches from where Dad was working with a small engine. The first drawer contained screwdrivers. The second drawer had pliers . . . and the padlock. The key was attached with a string. I closed the drawer and looked in the bottom one. Sandpaper and other odd things, which interested me not at all.

"Are you going to fix that all day?" I asked, trying to sound only casually interested.

"Probably," said Dad without looking up. "Was there something else you thought I should do?"

Yes.

"No," I said. "I just wondered."

"What's Angie doing?" asked Dad.

"Sleeping."

I wandered out of the shop and back toward the house. Larry was working by a tractor with his back to me. I glanced back at Dad. His head was bent over the engine. I changed directions quickly and ran around the shop to where I'd hidden the hammer, nails and oilcan. I couldn't get my bike without being seen, so I walked all the way.

Craig was waiting for me. We set to work right away, first closing the hole to the loft.

We had to cover it from the top, but to do it properly, we'd either have to jump down from the loft door or stay in there forever. We nailed half the hole shut as well as we could, using up almost every nail I brought, and then we climbed partway down the ladder, which was really just boards nailed to the wall. From there, we put a couple more boards up through the hole and laid them in place. It looked really good, but all anyone would have to do was bump his head against the loose boards, and he'd see what a secure cover we'd made. We weren't worried about a man getting through the hole even if he found it. Craig and I just managed to slither through, one after the other.

As I climbed back down the ladder, I noticed one of the rungs was loose. "We should pound that tighter while we have the hammer here," I suggested.

"No we shouldn't," said Craig. "We should take it off altogether. They probably wouldn't realize that was an opening if the ladder wasn't there."

"Especially in the dark," I agreed. "Great idea."

Pulling off the rungs wasn't difficult. We threw the boards in the junk pile by the old truck and went to cover the window.

"They could never get through this anyway," I said as I held one end of the piece of weather-beaten plywood Craig had brought.

"It's psychological," explained Craig. "If they see any holes or places to look out, they'll try harder to find a way to escape."

I handed Craig another nail, but it slipped out of my fingers as he reached for it. We'd had four when we started on the window, but Craig hit one crooked and it bent. Now we were down to two.

"We could pull some out of the rungs we took off the wall," I suggested.

"This'll do," said Craig. He gave the second nail a last bang with the hammer. "Now all the windows are covered," he said with satisfaction. "It'll make them feel more locked in."

He jumped quickly down from the pile, and I followed more slowly. "Looks like it might rain," said Craig, scanning the heavy clouds that had been building in the sky all day. "We'll be able to see the truck tracks in the mud then."

"We shouldn't need to," I said. "Not if we have the thieves locked in." I shivered as I looked at the barn. I would be very glad when tomorrow came.

# CHAPTER 12

D AD AND LARRY HAD JUST LEFT THE HOUSE AFTER COFFEE WHEN Rodos barked, signalling a vehicle entering the yard. Mum was upstairs sewing and the boys were outside somewhere, but I didn't stop playing the piano. It was probably someone to see Dad.

A minute or two later, the doorbell rang.

"I'll get it," yelled Angie. She dropped her doll on its head and ran out of the room. I followed more slowly.

"Is your mother home?" Mrs. Geller was asking when I reached the porch.

"She's upstairs. I'll get her," said Angie. She took off, shouting and leaving me to invite Mrs. Geller into the kitchen. I didn't want to, remembering her perfect house, but I had to. She must have been here before anyway, when Mum fitted her for her dress.

We made polite conversation about how I was enjoying the summer holidays. Then Mum came down, and I escaped outside.

A red and white soccer ball hit the step as I closed the door, then bounced into the flower bed. Nick tore past, scooped it up and headed back to the stretch of brown grass at the side of the house.

"Hey, no fair," yelled Trevor. "You're using your hands."

"That's okay," said another voice. "I'll be on your side. He'll

94

need his hands to beat us." Then Craig noticed me. "Hey, Marjorie. You're on Nick's team," he called.

"Hurry up."

When Mrs. Geller left the house, the parcel containing her dress under her arm, Craig said he'd walk home. He wanted to finish the game. Nick and I never had a chance against them, though Nick did score a couple of times and I got one goal. It was fun, though, right until Mum called us for supper and invited Craig to stay, too.

"Thanks, Mrs. Friesen," Craig replied.

As he went to phone his mother, I wondered if I could lay a towel on the worn patch on the kitchen floor, or would that look worse than it did already? Mum would probably say something like "What is that towel doing there?" and it would only draw attention to the floor anyway.

If Craig noticed the worn floor, he didn't show it. He sat beside Larry at the table and talked to the twins about baseball. Larry even joined in a couple times. I almost forgot to worry about our plans for the night.

"I'm going to check some fields," said Dad when he stood up from the table. "Would you like a ride home, Craig?"

"It's okay," said Craig. "I can walk."

"Say yes, Craig," I said. "Then I can drive. I haven't had a chance to drive since—"

"Since last week," said Dad with a smile. "Okay, you can drive as far as Gellers', if Craig trusts you, that is."

"Maybe now that we live in the country, I can learn to drive, too," said Craig as we climbed into the truck. "Except," he paused, "we don't have any fields to practice in. You're sure lucky to have a farm."

"You can borrow some of it," said Dad. "I'll talk to your father next time I see him. This trail right here is a good place to learn."

Driving was more fun than walking or riding a bike, but scarry, too. The trail wasn't very wide. I was glad there was little chance of meeting another vehicle.

I felt older sitting in the driver's seat, well forward so I could see over the dash. I was driving! Though I barely got over twenty kilometers an hour, we reached Craig's gate far too soon.

"Thanks for the supper and the ride," said Craig as he climbed out. "See you." He mouthed the words "at eleven."

I carefully backed the truck out of Craig's yard. Then Dad and I traded places.

"Looks like I survived another ordeal," said Dad as he shoved the truck into second. "I don't know what I'm going to do when Trevor and Nick are both learning to drive at once."

"I'll teach them," I offered. "I'll have my license years before they can get theirs."

"How long is it, now?" asked Dad. "Six years? You're almost ten, aren't you?"

"It's four and a half," I said indignantly. I started to tell him how old I was when I noticed his lips twitching and realized he was just teasing.

"How come you're so cheerful suddenly?" I pretended to grump. "At least when you're grouchy, you don't tease me."

"I'm feeling optimistic," said Dad. "Things seem to be getting better."

"What do you mean?" It came out louder than I meant to say it.

"The clouds, of course," said Dad, looking at me in surprise. "What did you think I meant? It looks like it just might rain."

His cheerfulness didn't help me at all. The men in the barn last night had been glad because things were going to be better, too.

Butterflies had made a permanent home in my stomach. Dad drove around checking for grasshoppers, drought damage and gophers. I sat beside him, wondering what thieves do when they learn someone has found their hiding place.

It was after eleven when I left the house dressed in a ski jacket and two pairs of sweat pants. There had still been a murmur of voices from Mum and Dad's bedroom, but I didn't dare wait any longer. The padlock was safe in my jacket pocket. I had snuck it out of the shop when Dad and I got back.

It was a wild night. Wind tore at the trees and rattled loose shingles on the shop. Something inside the barn banged, which was followed by the high-pitched squeal of a pig.

Rodos was getting so used to my nighttime trips that he came over immediately to get his cookies.

I stepped down to the ground and looked around. Dad's truck was parked by the house, along with the car. Larry's car appeared to be over by the bunkhouse. It was hard to tell, though. The night was darker than any I'd been out in lately. Heavy clouds hid the stars, and no lights were visible from any of the buildings. Even the lights from Dudley looked fainter and farther away than usual.

I wasn't taking any chances. Leaving my bike behind, I ducked around the corner of the house and hid myself in the row of trees circling the yard.

I couldn't feel the wind much in the trees, but it hit me with a blast when I stepped away from the shelter of the yard to head across a summer-fallow field. I turned my shoulder into the wind and burrowed my face in the collar of my jacket. Being off the trail meant I was less visible, but it also meant there was nothing to guide my steps.

Dust blew up from the field, stinging my cheeks and flinging grit in my eyes.

"You're late," Craig said when I arrived. He was crouching by the old truck, looking toward the highway. "They'll be here any minute."

"Too bad we couldn't try that door ahead of time," I worried. "I'm still afraid we won't get it closed while both the guys are in there."

"Don't worry," said Craig. "It's foolproof. They're not going to expect anything. They'll probably go in together to get the first boxes. We'll give them just enough time to get to the back of the barn. Then we slide the door shut and slap on the padlock. You *do* have the extra padlock?"

I patted my pocket. "Right here."

"Then we've got them," said Craig. "We can't miss."

I wish.

"Once they're locked in there, they won't be able to get out." I was sure of that, almost.

A vehicle was coming down the highway. It slowed at the corner to our trail and turned in. Its lights went out, but a moment later, they came back on. Thieves couldn't see in the dark any better than I could.

It went right past the barn toward our yard. The sound of the motor was lost in the wail of the wind.

The wind tore at our clothes and lashed our faces as we huddled among the junk between the truck and the barn, and waited for the thieves to return. An hour later, or maybe it was just a couple of minutes, the lights turned back toward us.

"You're sure no one saw you leave the house?" asked Craig, sounding almost as nervous as I felt.

"I didn't turn on any lights," I said. "I don't think anyone saw me. Do you think we should hide farther away?"

There was no time to decide. The truck had arrived. It's lights shone past the barn as it swung around, illuminating the front of the old truck and a discarded wheel rim just a step away from my foot. As the headlights continued in their arc, I peeked around the corner. The truck was backing up to the door. I edged backward, toward the rear of the barn. My heart was beating so loud I was afraid the thieves would hear it even inside their truck.

The motor died, and the lights went out at the same time. I strained to hear what was happening through the howling of the wind. The men climbed out of the truck; a door slammed shut. I could hear them talking together but couldn't make out any words. Then one of them laughed.

Craig tugged on my arm. "Let's go," he whispered so quietly that I felt the words more than I heard them.

I inched along the wall after Craig, grateful that the noisy wind covered the sounds of shifting junk beneath our feet. It was a relief to feel solid ground again as we neared the back of the barn.

Craig rounded the corner first. I wanted to stop. I couldn't see anything, not even Craig in front of me. There was so much topsoil in the air that the lights of Dudley were no longer visible.

I stopped moving. What was I doing? It was crazy. They'd probably kill us. There wasn't a hope we could catch them.

A hand grabbed my arm. I was so frightened I couldn't even scream. I knew the thieves would check behind the barn. I knew they would catch us.

# CHAPTER 13

"Hurry up, Marjorie. We're going to miss our chance." Craig tugged on my arm, dragging me after him. I pulled myself free.

"I can walk," I whispered furiously. "Leave me alone."

"Then hurry up!"

I ran my hand across the barn wall to guide me along the back, around the corner and up the side. Beneath the window we'd crawled through so many times, I tripped on our pile of stones and fence posts. I froze.

Again Craig jerked my arm impatiently.

"Come on!" he whispered. "They're opening the padlock. You're lucky they had trouble with the tailgate of the truck, or they'd have the barn empty already."

A prolonged, eerie screech drowned him out. They had opened the door. Oiling hadn't affected the noise it made. How would we ever get it closed in time?

I bumped into Craig. We'd reached the end of the wall. Turning the corner would put us only steps from the door we had to close.

But with the sound of the wind, how would we ever know when they were at the back of the barn?

I brushed past Craig and peered around the corner. I couldn't even make out the shape of their truck.

A flash of lightning split the sky. I drew back swiftly, flattening myself against the barn wall. Had anyone seen me in that flash? I hadn't been looking at the barn or the rear of the truck. All I had seen in that brief moment of light was the cab of the truck with the door standing open.

The door was open. The door was open. The words ran through my mind as if they mattered. The interior light didn't work. That's why I didn't know the door was open before.

The keys! Dad always left the keys in the truck. Had these men done the same?

The sound of far-off thunder died away just in time for me to catch the muffled thump of a box of chemicals being placed in the truck. Craig tugged on my arm. "Get ready," he whispered in my ear.

I ignored him. Without stopping to think I darted toward the truck.

What if a bolt of lightning flashed and they saw me?

I banged into the open door, stepped sideways and reached into the truck. I felt the dash beside the steering wheel. Nothing there. I checked the column. No key. I reached past the steering wheel and felt the dash on the other side.

It wasn't a ring of keys, just one by itself. I snatched it in such a hurry that it slipped from my nervous fingers.

I felt around on the floor in the dirt and gravel and sunflower seed shells. Just as I touched something metal, the truck lurched. Oh no! They were putting more chemicals into the back!

I was shocked at how quickly they could walk to the back of the barn, pick up a carton of chemicals and return to the truck.

I froze, praying they wouldn't come to the cab for something.

They didn't.

The metal I'd found was just a bottle cap. My fingers moved in a bigger circle.

At last! The key. I jammed it into my pocket with the padlock I'd brought from home.

The truck moved again as another box of chemicals joined those already in the back. I shrank against the cab of the truck.

Another bolt of lightning lit the sky. In the brief light, I saw Craig's terrified face peering around the corner of the barn. As darkness settled again, I dashed back to him, arriving just as a roll of thunder drowned out the moan of the wind.

"What were you doing?" Craig whispered angrily. "We missed our chance."

"We don't have a chance," I whispered back. "They're too fast."

He didn't answer but peered around the corner again.

"Now!" he said suddenly and disappeared. I stared blankly into the darkness, then realized what he was doing.

He was already pushing on the door when I joined him. We shoved harder, and the door screamed in protest.

Though the wind was loud, the door was louder. I couldn't hear any identifiable sounds from inside the barn, but I was sure the thieves were coming.

"Faster," urged Craig. "Push harder. Get your padlock ready."

I couldn't push harder and get the padlock out at the same time. I was already pushing as hard as I could. I could feel slivers from the rotting wood stabbing my bare hands, but I kept on pushing.

The door reached the end of the track and Craig tried to close the hasp as I fumbled for the padlock.

"They're moving the door!" cried Craig. "Marjorie, help!"

I pushed, trying to keep it closed, but the men on the other side were bigger and stronger.

"Run," I yelled as the door started to open. I turned but took only one step before someone grabbed me.

"Kids!" exclaimed a surprised voice over my head. One hand grabbed my arm and pulled me against him. His other hand, in a sickeningly dirty glove, covered most of my face.

"Keep his eyes covered," yelled the man holding me. "We don't want them seeing us." As if we could see anything in this darkness anyway.

He was holding me so tightly my ribs hurt, and I started to gag from the smell of his glove. I couldn't see or hear anything.

Lightning flashed, but it didn't help at all. At the same instant, the skies opened up and rain started to fall.

The rain seemed to push the thieves into motion. I felt myself being swung off the ground and carried into the barn. What were they going to do with us?

My captor walked a long ways. It must have been to the very back. Then he stopped and dropped me. My feet touched the floor first, but I overbalanced and fell backward. "Don't try to leave!" he warned before turning away.

There was a thud and a scrambling noise, and I knew Craig had joined me.

"Shouldn't we tie them up?" said the voice I had recognized the night before.

Larry.

"What with?" returned the first man. "We don't have time to get any rope if we're going to get this stuff to your brother before daybreak. They should be okay for a day or two. Maybe they'll break out eventually. By then it won't matter."

They had left us in one of the stalls, probably the last one in the barn, across from the stall with the chemicals . . . the same one I'd hidden in the night before.

"Did he hurt you?" I whispered to Craig.

"I'm okay," said Craig, but he didn't sound okay at all. He sounded scared. Just like I felt.

I thought of Mum at home in bed. Maybe she'd woken up

when it started to rain. She'd be lying there, listening to the rain, thankful that it had finally come, never guessing that I wasn't safe in bed as well.

And Dad. He was at home, too. I was sure of that, now. The relief inside me was so great I almost forgot to be scared. Almost.

I moved over to the wall, and Craig came and sat beside me. We waited, shoulder to shoulder, leaning against the rough boards of the barn and listening to the rain drumming on the walls. Listening to the wind whistling through the cracks in the barn. Listening to the thunder.

Listening as footsteps trudged back and forth, back and forth. Picking up chemicals, putting them in the truck. Picking up chemicals, putting them in the truck.

A sudden light shone in my eyes, blinding me.

"I see you're being—" a voice above the flashlight began and then stopped. Larry had recognized me. Now what?

The flashlight clicked off and I heard him swear. What would he do now? Would he know I recognized him? Maybe not. The flashlight hadn't shone in his face.

I could only hope.

Larry went out to the alley, and I heard the men talking, but the storm muffled their voices.

A moment later, the door screeched shut with its now-familiar protest.

Our plan had almost worked. Someone was locked in the barn.

# CHAPTER 14

"**H**URRY UP!" I WHISPERED TO CRAIG. "WE HAVEN'T GOT MUCH time. We have to get out of here."

"What's the hurry?" asked Craig. "They're not coming back."

"We'll get them yet," I promised. "Just hurry."

I felt my way down the alley toward the stall with the window. "They'll be back within minutes," I said. "I have their truck key."

"Way t'go!" exclaimed Craig.

We couldn't hear anything except the storm, but I could imagine what the men were doing. They would both climb in the truck. The driver would reach for the key. It wouldn't be there. He'd probably check his pockets. Then he'd fumble around on the floor, thinking it had dropped, maybe getting the flashlight to see for sure.

I bumped into the manger, then quickly climbed in. Craig started pounding with his fists on the plywood covering the window. I pushed. We'd used long nails, but just two. I could feel the board starting to give.

The men had probably left the truck and were looking for the key on the ground . . . in the mud. It wouldn't be long before they figured out where it was.

My shoulders ached from pushing, and the slivers in my hands burned. I dropped my arms to my sides.

"I can't do it."

"You have to," said Craig. "Let's trade sides."

We switched places. I could tell by the feel of the board that Craig's pounding had moved it more than my pushing. I started pounding, too, grateful that the wind and rain and occasional thunder covered the noise.

Then came the sound I'd been waiting for. It scared me anyway. The opening of the sliding door. The noise didn't last long this time; they must have just opened it enough to get through.

With one final desperate push the board gave way and fell to the ground.

I grabbed the windowsill and hoisted myself up. I had barely squeezed through when Craig joined me outside in the pouring rain.

"Come on, you little creeps. Game's up. Give us the key." The voice came from inside the barn. I didn't hear Larry, but I hoped he'd gone in, too. If he hadn't . . .

There was no more slow sneaking. We tore around the corner, our feet slipping on the wet ground, and shoved against the door.

It was easier this time. Just a short push before the door slid into place. Craig pulled the hasp over the eye on the door. I grabbed the padlock from my pocket and slipped it on.

Just in time. Both men were on the other side of the door, yelling and shoving. How long would the rotting wood of the door stand it? How long before they pushed the door out of the bottom track enough to crawl out?

I burrowed my cold, sore hands into my pockets. And felt a key.

The truck! "Get out of the way," I yelled to Craig, and ran for the cab.

It started on the first try. I shoved it into reverse and backed straight toward the barn, not stopping till the bumper thudded against the door. They could push and shove all they wanted. The door wasn't going to move.

The truck door flew open as soon as I turned off the motor. "Move over," Craig yelled. "It's wet out here."

"Somebody has to phone the police," I reminded him as I moved. "Too bad I can't take the truck, but I don't trust that door." I wasn't sure I trusted any of that barn. We escaped from it fast enough.

"I pounded the wood back on the window," said Craig. "It won't hold up if they try pushing it off, but I'm sure they're too big to get through anyway."

"I hope you're right," I said. And in case he wasn't, I locked the truck doors.

Craig ran home through the pouring rain to phone the police. I shivered in the locked truck, pulling slivers out of my hands with my teeth. What were the men in the barn doing now? Ripping boards off the walls and escaping through the back? Climbing out a window? Starting the place on fire?

I was sure of one thing. They weren't sitting on the floor waiting for someone to let them out. They were using their flashlight to find a way to escape. And they would find it. They had too much to lose if they didn't.

How long would the police take?

A beam of light lit the trail. It stayed too long to be lightning. I twisted in my seat. Twin headlights were coming up the trail from the highway, swerving a bit on the wet surface but coming quickly for all that.

It was too soon to be the police.

I checked that the doors really were locked and slid down on the floor beneath the steering wheel. Maybe someone looking in the window wouldn't see me.

The vehicle stopped beside the truck. Doors opened and

slammed shut. Someone tried the truck door. I kept my head down, thankful my ski jacket was a dark color.

A light shone into the cab of the truck and I shrunk even closer to the floor.

"She's gone," yelled Craig. "I left her right in the truck and she's gone." The light disappeared.

I crawled out from under the dash and opened the truck door.

"I'm still here," I said sheepishly. "I thought you were more thieves, so I hid on the floor."

"That was a smart move," said Craig's father.

"The RCMP are coming," interrupted Craig. "It took three calls before I got hold of a real live person, but she said she'd radio the closest car."

Craig turned his flashlight on again and shone it toward the barn. "What do you think they're doing in there?" he wondered.

"Trying to get out," I said. "What else? I hope the police hurry. I don't think tomorrow afternoon will be soon enough."

"Would you like a ride home?" asked Mr. Geller.

"Are you kidding?" I asked. Leave the most exciting thing that had ever happened to me? Not likely.

"Okay," said Mr. Geller. "But I'll turn the car so we can watch the barn while we wait out of the rain."

If Larry and his friend did escape, they weren't going to take the evidence with them. I locked the door again, and checked that the key was safe in my pocket. Then Craig and I ran through the rain to join his dad in the front seat of the car.

The wind died down, but the rain continued, drumming steadily on the roof of the car. There were occasional banging sounds from the barn, which meant the men hadn't given up.

When I next saw headlights come up the slope from the highway, I didn't even think about it being more thieves. The police car pulled up beside us, and two officers stepped out. They joined us in Mr. Geller's car while we explained what had happened.

One of the officers had been at the elevator in Dudley the day after the robbery there. He wasn't nearly as pleased as I thought he would be. "You could have been hurt trying something like that," he said when we were done.

"But we weren't," said Craig.

"I think you kids did just great," said the policewoman. "But you took a big chance."

"I know," I said. "I had to."

# EPILOGUE

*Dear Pam,*

*Before you read this letter, read the newspaper clippings. They will tell you how brave I am so I don't have to brag.*

*Pretty good picture, eh? Since the police got stuck trying to drive the truck full of chemicals, it was still there when the photographer came. She wanted us to put on our muddy clothes again, but luckily Mum had already washed mine.*

*You'd think Dad would have been overjoyed. He wasn't. He reminded me that he'd told us not to go in the barn. He's going to start tearing it down as soon as it's dry enough to drive on the trail.*

*I wouldn't tell anyone else because it's really stupid, but for the longest time, I actually wondered if Dad was the thief. He kept going to these late meetings, and he was really grouchy for a while, I guess because it was so dry out, or maybe because Larry wasn't working very hard, but you know what I thought. It didn't help when Craig saw Dad's truck at the barn once with stolen chemicals in it, and I found one of Dad's hats there. It turns out Larry took Dad's truck without telling him some- times, and once he took Dad's hat by mistake and lost it in the barn. Dad didn't even know his hat was gone. He just wears whichever one he grabs first.*

*Craig and I thought maybe Jack Kingsley was the thief, but he bought some of the chemicals from Larry thinking they were*